Advanced Praise for King

It's often said that the Bible is the most violent book ever written. This rich tapestry of tales draws on Biblical slaughter, cruelty, and mayhem from ancient times to the modern day - a theme anthology that not only keeps you interested in the theme, but makes you look at the source material with new eyes.

Poppy Z. Brite

Richly detailed--and thoroughly creepy--retellings of biblical stories (some familiar, some not so). Powerful imagination at work here

Gerri Leen

Dark and enticing, the stories in King David and the Spiders from Mars explore Biblical themes with a paradoxical combination of religious irreverence and respect for the literary richness of the texts. Marked by lush prose, often disturbing at a gut level, these are stories that stay with you.

Ilana Teitelbaum

I thoroughly enjoyed this collection. Tim Lieder has gathered together a great mix of stories, each wonderfully crafted. It was hard to put down.

Paul McAvoy, Whispers of Wickedness

King David and The Spiders from Mars isn't a collection of stories about ancient times. The authors within take classical Biblical tales and themes and spin them out to tales of love, denial and piety that include as their backdrop modern day Brooklyn and the outer reaches of space. This is not your Sunday School Teacher's morning lessons; this is uncharted territory of the divine. Proceed and reap this book's rewards at your own risk.

Thomas Deja

Praise for *She Nailed a Stake Through His Head*

This darkly fascinating anthology of nine stories shows humans trembling in the presence of mighty, unknowable powers and their predatory servants. In Gerri Leen's "Whither Thou Goest," Ruth is revealed to be a psychic leech, giving freshly disturbing meaning to her touching vow never to leave her aged mother-in-law. Jesus' exhortation to drink His blood is taken literally by a congregation of vampires in D.K. Thompson's "Last Respects." A modern Daniel finds that his gift of prophecy can serve the greedy gods of a multinational security corporation in Daniel Kayson's "Babylon's Burning," and Stephen M. Wilson's "Swallowed!" puts a Lovecraftian spin on the tale of Jonah and the whale. Brief but potent, these stories are recommended for readers with very strong nerves.

Publishers Weekly (Starred Review)

This book takes the Bible back from those right-wing fascists who want to rewrite it as a tedious book of loving and caring. These are stories as bawdy and lustful and horrifying as the original Good Book -- wild sex, savage violence, horrific curses...and, of course, vampires.

Matthue Roth, author, performance poet, Torah badass

You don't need to be Jewish or Christian to appreciate She Nailed a Stake Through His Head: Tales of Biblical Terror. Still, you may find yourself groping for a religious icon for protection given the unholy places these weird tales will take you.

Erin O'Riordan

King David

and the Spiders from Mars

Edited by Tim Lieder

Dybbuk Press
New York, NY
March 2014

Printed in New York

ISBN: 0-9766546-8-7
13-number ISBN: 978-0-9766546-8-1
Library of Congress Control Number: 2013949451

Copyright History
Introduction © 2013 Tim Lieder
"Moving Nameless" © 2002 by Sonya Taaffe. Originally published in *Not One of Us* #27, edited by John Benson, March 2002.
"The Chronicles of Aliyat Son of Aliyat from the Chronicles of the Kings of Ashdod" © 2011 by Alter Reiss. Originally appeared in *Historical Lovecraft*, edited by Silvia Moreno-Garcia and Paula R. Stiles, published by Innsmouth Free Press
"Good King David" © 2014. Jeff Chapman
"Chabad of Innsmouth" © 2014 Marsha Morman
"Three Young Men" © 2014 Romie Stott
"God Box" © 2014 Lyda Morehouse
"The Sons of Zeruiah" © 2014 Megan Arkenberg

Cover designed by Jacob Fine
Cover painting is David with the Head of Goliath by Amerighi da Caravaggio.

Dedicated to Dr. Libbat Shaham

Table of Contents

Introduction

Helen Keller overcame diversity and became fodder for inspirational posters and tasteless jokes. Opera is for snobs. Pop music is for idiots. War & Peace is the GREAT BOOK, more of a reading challenge than actual entertainment. The Bible is either the cornerstone of all morality or a boring little book used by religious zealots and hypocrites to quote for arguments.

This kind of cultural shorthand can be so pervasive, that you don't even know when you're relying on it. I was in my twenties when I learned that Helen Keller was a radical socialist who attributed her success to her family's wealth. Opera can be bloodier and crazier than the best Tarantino films. Popular music can be just as transcendent and beautiful as jazz or classical music.

The Bible suffers most from cultural shorthand. Since the Bible is the basis for two major world religions, many approach it with a false reverence where all ambiguity and tension vanishes. When Thomas Bowdler put out his Family Shakespeare book, he dealt with the troubling parts (supposedly not suitable for women and children) by removing them entirely. In the case of the Bible, bowdlerizing is unnecessary. Boring translations, purposefully inane commentaries and superficial interpretations have managed to convince people that they already know the Bible so why bother reading it?

What is the Book of Job about? If you answered that Job is a good man who suffers, keeps the faith and eventually gets everything back, mazel tov! You know about 3% of the book and you completely misinterpreted the ending. You might as well say that MacBeth is a play about a Scottish dude that gets his head cut off or that Wuthering Heights is a love story. It's not entirely your fault. The reductionist

9

version inspires great sermons. Few religious leaders are going to highlight the many passages with Job calling God a sadistic asshole, much less God's sarcastic and rather brilliant response.

It should not feel revolutionary or blasphemous to approach the Bible as literature. The Bible is funny, psychotic, contradictory and bizarre. That's what makes it awesome. Granted, the Bible can get dull, especially for people who don't have an interest in following Jewish law or building a temple in their backyard (or Jerusalem for that matter); however, the Bible is also an ancient text that takes in centuries of literary and social history and distills it into a collection that is at turns reverential, hilarious and profound, but always built upon a tension of a religious framework that requires constant dialogue and dynamic engagement.

Both this book and its predecessor, *She Nailed a Stake Through His Head*, come from a place of profound reverence and love for the Bible. In the previous book, I mentioned how much I was shocked and delighted to discover that the Bible can be existentialist, erotic, historical, apocalyptic and full of poop jokes like Beelzebub (aka Lord of the Flies, aka the shit pile where all the flies are congregating).

As I learned from *She Nailed a Stake Through His Head*, the cultural shorthand associated with the Bible also applies to Bible themed short story collections. Many customers assumed that the collection was either monotheist indoctrination or pure blasphemy. I would have argued with them, but they were giving me money. However, if you are reading this introduction, it's important to note that the book is collected with appreciation for great literature. It is not meant to convert anyone to any religion. Nor is it meant to trash anyone's faith. Furthermore the stories are meant to stand on their own merits. If you know nothing about King David, Joab, Tamar, Daniel or Absalom, you might miss a couple of references, but I chose stories that are brilliant on their own merits. They are not puzzles to challenge Bible nerds. However, if you like the stories enough that you want to explore further, most of them are based on tales from the Book of Samuel. If you can find a good translation, definitely read it.

Moving Nameless
By Sonya Taaffe

"Don't be afraid," Adam whispered. In the sloping afternoon light she could see the sweat shining on his cheekbones, half from summer, half from her nearness; he had shaved that morning and already there was shadow grained beneath his skin. She wanted to touch him, put one hand alongside his jaw until the faint sandpaper sensation rasped against her palm and the tips of her fingers. If she tilted her face, she could make their mouths meet. But sorrow like stone weighted her movements, dragged at her blood, and instead she stood very still as Adam murmured again, "Don't be afraid." His reassurance made her smile. He was the one afraid: shy and fearful of getting it wrong, not pleasing her, scaring her away. What could she fear? He would not hurt her. He could not. But she would hurt him; that was the way of the world, and her bones ached with the knowledge. The old mantelpiece clock, now transferred to a sideboard in the miniature kitchen, ticked out time in the stillness softened by their breathing. She did not know how many seconds she had left. Despairing, desiring, she took Adam's hands in her own.

He had been showing her his apartment — not really his apartment, his grandfather's, but his grandfather was visiting Adam's aunt in Topeka and his parents had allowed him the month's experimental use of the three rooms and storage closet — and now they stood together in the sunlit living room, as careful and awkward with one another as all first-time lovers. Earlier they had eaten Thai food across the street from the bookstore where Adam worked, browsed the used book shop where Adam spent all his paychecks, and walked back to his grandfather's apartment with their hands clasped and swinging between them. Nothing had happened; she was still a little surprised. Over their heads the sky had simmered rich with the season, clouds blossoming out of the haze feather-white against heat-soaked blue. Their shadows had paced one another on the sidewalk. Asphalt stuck to their shoes.

Fortunately the apartment was in the basement; shadowed, but not subterranean, and light streamed over the floor when Adam flung up the shades. For a while they talked, as Adam showed her pieces of his life and his grandparents' that had settled about the apartment: sculptures his grandfather had done before his eyesight went, old books that slid household to household depending on who wanted to read what, photographs of Adam and his family at varying ages, childish drawings, dried flowers, detritus of memory that she absorbed through his words.

"It's amazing that your parents trust you this much," she remarked. "Not to mention your grandfather. Handing over the apartment to an adolescent — You must really get along."

"Yeah." Adam shrugged, unimpressed and a little embarrassed. "They're good people. I like them. How about yours?"

"Oh," she said, quietly, "we don't talk much anymore."

"I'm sorry." They were sitting side-by-side on the couch, beneath a charcoal sketch of Adam's grandmother holding her first child, Adam's father, in her arms. In the blurred lines she could find familiar traces of Adam: broad, raised cheekbones, peaked eyes, mouth that widened easily into a sharing smile; unbeautiful in repose but more than attractive when animated. Roughed in, his grandmother's hair was braided and piled about her head. Adam's hair sprang over his shoulders, dark and unruly. He looked nothing like his maternal great-uncle, for whom he had been named. She could grow to like him very much.

Suddenly it hurt to breathe; it hurt to hear Adam's sympathy. "It's all right," she managed. "I'm doing fine." But she was not, she was lying, and Adam did not know. He did not even know to look for the lies, as when he called "Eva!" because he wanted her to see a book he had found, because that was the name she had not denied when he guessed at it. He liked the cheerful, impossible allusion. She did not have the heart to discourage him; it had been his own name that first caught her attention.

He looked nothing like his oldest namesake, and the other countless Adams she had met in all the years since as one human man looks like another. Adam

Harrow, the great-uncle who had been her friend, had been earnest and red-headed — gone springing white in later photographs, an unblown dandelion with a shy smile — thin and bespectacled, the very archetype of a weedy scholar. In fact he had been a newspaper editor, a well-read one, and had known her name before she told him. But an earnest short-sighted editor had not helped her, nor the banker who had borne his name before him, nor the courtier, the alchemist, the monk, the madman . . . After the first few millennia, she had learned to disregard the years, but she had never learned to disregard the pain.

Whether she thought Adam Loukides could help her, or whether she merely felt the hopeless smile cross her face as soon as he introduced himself and she knew she had made her decision, she did not know. But the irony was wonderful, and he was cheerful and meticulous when she asked after a book that had caught her curiosity. "Robert Graves' Hebrew Myths? Out of print," Adam apologized, "but I know this great used book store around the corner, and I can run over and check and see if they have it. Do you like Robert Graves? I've only read his Claudius books. You know, the Roman ones. Only because I'm a Derek Jacobi fan, really, which is kind of sad . . . my mother was a classics major in college." From the moment he spoke, she loved the sound of his voice: informal rambling phrases said with crisp ease, a classically trained actor with a high-school vocabulary. "Look, I'm off work in fifteen minutes. Do you want to run over to the bookstore with me? We can get lunch from the Thai place — they've got amazing coconut soup — or there's this place that does sandwiches, really nice ones, and we can sort of poke around. There's a plethora of restaurants in this area. Not enough bookstores, but a lot of restaurants." Suddenly shy, he flushed beneath his fair olive skin and said almost too loudly and too quickly, "How's that sound?"

Already she liked him; and because she knew it was hopeless, she was safe in her liking. Adam's eyes were the color of ancient amber, dark until the light tipped into them and clarified to a smoky, concentrated almond. His fingers tapped an arrhythmic tattoo on the countertop. Before he could speak again, she nodded. "It sounds wonderful," she said. "I'd love to."

She did not find a copy of her book that day, although she had a very nice sandwich eaten on the green outside the library, but she had found Adam. "Adam Yves Loukides," he said grandly, gesturing with his own half-eaten sandwich, "and if that isn't a name to make you cringe, I don't know what is. My parents were trying to name me for each side of the family. Pity that everyone in my family has names no one's ever heard of."

"I think most people will recognize Adam," she said dryly.

"Fine, but Yves? The last person I saw named Yves was in a medieval mystery."

"Sorry."

King David and the Spiders from Mars

"Don't apologize to me," Adam sulked, sprawled full-length in the sunlight with half a tomato sandwich in one hand and the other folded as a pillow behind his head, "complain to my parents!" Then he grinned. When she came back to the bookstore the next day, it might have been for the care he took over her book, his sandwich recommendations and his speeches about names, or even his kind, spontaneous grin that eased a little of the worry collecting cold beneath her heart; but regardless, she came back, and Adam was very pleased to see her.

A week later they finally made it to the Thai restaurant, where she tried the coconut soup and agreed that yes, it was amazing, and almost destroyed her sinuses asking for red curry extra hot. After that, he invited her home. It was an idyll, a dream. She had loved every swift-running second of it. Now she stood beside the glass-topped coffee table where she had risen to escape his kindness — his understanding that could never really understand — holding Adam's hands in fear and tenderness. He had put on one of his grandfather's records for her, Benny Goodman's famous 1938 Carnegie Hall version of "Sing, Sing, Sing," but it had ended almost ten minutes ago. The melody was still going around in her head. She was listening to the clock tick.

Clocks and watches were useless to her, long before their invention; she measured time in the silent geologic roar of cracking continents and rising seas, mountains lathed to desert, stone pried from stone, the

18

winds that swept from every quarter of the globe save that one forgotten place. She had not forgotten it. She never forgot. But mortals forget, men forget, Adam had not been able to find Graves' book and did not know her name. Scant inches from her face, amber eyes fractured with the light filtering through the dust-glazed panes, he was trying to comfort her, trying to kiss her, drawn to her for reasons he would never be able to explain. She knew them, of course. Made for love, to love, she could not help but want to hold him; she could not hate, only sorrow. She was sorrowing now.

Adam drew one hand free of her clasp, combed fingers through her hair; lifted the dense fall from her face and touched the angle of her cheekbone with his lips. He was very gentle. With equal gentleness, she turned her face and closed the distance between them with her mouth.

Adam's body tensed against hers, eager, undemanding, and she felt more than she heard the soft noise he made under his breath as her hands slid to the nape of his neck. Her mouth tasted of nothing at all. Did he find that odd? Lost in the taste and texture of him, she could not tell; his mouth moved on hers, his hands traced her body; blurred with the scant distance between them, she saw the dark fan of his eyelashes closed against his cheekbones. Between her fingers, his hair curled soft and wiry, and his skin heated beneath her fingertips. There were tears packed behind her eyes. With the certainty of millennia, she kissed Adam and waited for it to happen.

It came like a galvanic flash, a lightning stroke driving into him through her body, and it smashed them apart. His head jerked back and she knew he had seen, she saw it in his eyes, not the last sight of a dying man but the last image of dying love. Imagination flayed her, skin peeling from flesh, veins stranding from muscle, disclosing blood that seeped, saliva that spilled, jellied globe of one beautiful disconnected eye; he saw her constructed from marrow to breath, the cartilage fretwork of her throat knotting with ligaments, ribcage filled and pulsing to the spasmodic double beat of heart and lungs, hair sown in her scalp over the thin zigzag bones. Metamorphosis without physical change, realization and recognition: the rooted stubs of bone his tongue explored, the sag of glands his hands cupped, wet meat, slick bone, membrane and gristle waxed with fat and corded with sinews, all the fascinating sickening strata of flesh that slid beneath her faultless skin. Adam made a sound in his throat — not the same noise, so much the same noise that she felt the wrench like bones breaking about her heart — and let her go. One minute their mouths were fastened, the next he stood halfway across the room, disgust smeared and stamped on his features so clearly that even he felt it and tried to smooth it away, wiping both hands over his face, shaking, too shocked even to swear.

"God," he said when he could speak, the words heaving out of him, "oh, God. Eva —"

"Don't call me that." In his moment of understanding she had drawn into herself, receded from beneath the margin of her pristine skin. She felt a physical distance between herself and her bones, her flesh and the air that pressed against it; she moved as jerkily as a marionette as she got herself to the couch and folded onto it. The ancient sorrow ate at her breath and she gasped a little, between words. She whispered, "It's not my name. I don't have a name."

Adam leaned against the wall. The blood had run out of his face, leaving the bones pressed white against the skin: startled out of himself into a stranger's look. He swallowed shock and croaked, "What are you?"

Her face bent in a smile without humor. "That book knows, the one we couldn't find. The nameless virgin. Adam's second wife. After Lilith left, threw him over for Ashmedai on the shores of the Red Sea, God made — You have to call her a woman, she wasn't anything else. But not a woman like Lilith was a woman, like Eve was a woman, made out of earth or flesh. He made her out of nothing, out of his will, before Adam's very eyes: bones, muscles, tendons, flesh. Piece by piece. Layer over layer. You saw. What's inside everyone, that's all, but Adam had never looked into a living body. They didn't have *Gray's Anatomy* then. And he saw her and sickened. He couldn't touch her. So Eve was made while he slept, so that he should not see her creation; and on waking he managed to forget what he had learned from the sight of the second woman, the forgotten one, the surface of Eve's beauty so enthralled him. Maybe God helped him to forget. God was kind to him. The second helpmeet — Some people say God destroyed her. Some people say he only made her leave Eden. Gone out into the world like Lilith; not like Lilith, really. Lilith had her anger and her beauty, her immortality and her power. The nameless woman had beauty and immortality only. No gifts, those. Nor did she fall, like Eve. Adam wouldn't get near her: how could she ever leave her innocence? No one touches her. No one can bear it." Her voice crumbled under the burning tears. "I can't touch anyone. Ever."

"Eva . . ." Adam swayed; his precise, slangy voice wavered and he sat abruptly on the floor, collapsible as a string-cut puppet himself, to sink his head forward and shudder. "I'm sorry. I'm sorry. I didn't mean that . . . I don't know what to call you now."

"There isn't anything to call me. In any language. I've learned so many," she whispered, "so many." Of all those who had tried to touch her, men and woman both, the kind ones were the worst. She did not care when a groping hand stiffened as though stung, a mouth rummaging over hers yelled in shock, but she flinched from the anguish scoring Adam Loukides' face: that he should see her suffering and could not ease it. He could not even press her shoulder in a friend's caress, could not even hold her hands as she wept. "No name. Nothing. God made me so."

"I don't believe in God." His voice shivered on the edge of crying. "But people breathe, bleed, shit, all of that, I know that; I've got hydrochloric acid rattling around in my stomach, it's no big deal; but I couldn't, I, I saw — I saw you, Eva!" he cried, and she did not stop to correct the name. "I shouldn't feel like this, I shouldn't. It's not reasonable. But I can't — I don't understand it. It's not God. I don't know what it is."

"God or no God," she said, desolate, definite, "what does it matter? My memories are the story. What I remember happened in someone else's words, the words of the storyteller who took the tale of Adam and Eve and filled in the spaces, the words of the man who translated the midrash, the words of the editor who proofed the book for publication, and all the generations in between and after — but still it happened to me. My creation is the story." Sunlight warmed her shoulders; it did nothing for the ache of ice branching in her veins. She closed her eyes. She did not want to see if Adam was looking at her in fascination, away from her in revulsion. In his eyes she would see the knowledge of the first Adam, what he had learned from her and then forgotten: another kind of fall. She murmured to the red-washed darkness behind her eyelids, "God doesn't have to exist. Only the tale. Only me."

"So change the tale. Tell the story differently. Say the nameless woman, Adam's second wife, found a boy she loved who worked at a bookstore and spent the rest of her life with him. Say she kissed him and nothing happened except what's supposed to happen when two people who're attracted to one another kiss." Hope made his voice raw. "Tell the story that way."

She shouted, "Do you think I haven't tried that?" There was no anger in her voice, she could not be angry, only a great and tearing grief. "Your great-uncle tried it. He wrote stories — not very well, but he loved doing it — and he wrote me a story where we stayed together until our deaths, side by side in the same bed, breathing out our last breath on the same sigh. And here . . . Here I am, Adam. Adam, if I could touch you—" She bent her head into her hands and tasted the tears that ran between her fingers. "I don't know how not to want to."

She heard the catch of his breath, as it struck him: the ceaseless journey, a different country every time, a different face, a different courtship, but always the endless repetition of the same story over and over past all human limits; but she was not human, not mortal, lost to Eden before its gates closed. Adam's first failure that had stamped her into this changeless mold still held true.

Adam Loukides, her dark-haired garrulous Adam of the bookstore, whispered from across the room, "What now?"

"I don't know." Now she lifted her head, ran a hand over her face and pulled tear-wet strands out of her eyes; he was not watching her with horror, nor with interest, but steadily and with pain. "People love me. And they are always hurt. Everything we've ever tried" — she and all the thousand thousand friends, lovers, companions that might have been — "has never worked. Each one thinks he'll be the one to change things, she'll break the curse, we'll live happily ever after. Nothing changes. Our lives go on. Adam, I have to leave. It will get worse. You can look at me now, but soon you won't be able to do even that. You won't be able to stand being in the same room as me. Soon you won't want to think of me; and then, like the first Adam, you'll wake one morning and forget. You'll never know I was here. Or if you remember, you'll remember only that something terrible happened, that it didn't work out in some awful, sickening way. Like the first Adam. Only I remember."

"I . . . I understand." Adam's mouth worked over a word he did not dare to say. Then he rose, clambering to his feet with one hand against the wall, and crossed the room in hesitant strides. "Come on. I want to look at you. I want to remember."

"You don't."

"No, I do. I mean, it hurts somehow, to see you. But I keep thinking, if I look hard enough, it'll stop hurting. Like eating that red curry you ordered, remember? I thought the inside of my mouth was going to peel off. That's a disgusting image . . . But I kept eating it, because I figured it couldn't get any worse. And shoveling in the rice. And maybe it worked, because I still have my tongue and all my teeth . . ." Rambling as when she first met him, he stooped and held out one hand, and she took it to pull herself to her feet.

25

He flinched. His hand snapped out of hers, his feet took him two stumbling steps backwards before he realized what he was doing. Immediately a brick-red flush slammed into his face: shame and guilt burning beneath the skin. "I'm sorry," he gasped, "Christ, I'm sorry. I thought — I hoped—"

"It's all right," she answered. Of course it was not. "It's not your fault." He hovered at her elbow as she left the living room, passed the bedroom and the kitchen where the light fell in late dust-grained slants through the high windows; he unlocked the door for her and followed her up the stairs, close enough that she could feel his presence stir the air against her skin; but he did not try to touch her again. Though she heard Adam make soft choked sounds from time to time, she was not crying. Her heart had broken open, and all her tears run out.

On the steps, he paused in the doorway and raised one hand in something between a farewell wave and a summons; the gesture hesitated, and he let his hand fall. She was already walking away when she heard his voice and turned.

"Come back." A sallow ghost of his sympathetic grin twitched at his mouth. "You know where I am. I work all through August, and in the fall I'm back at college. I'm easy to find." Tears glassed his amber eyes, turned illegible black by the fall of shadow from the yew hedge beside the door. "If . . . if I don't remember you, tell me. I'm not your first Adam. I want to see you again."

26

"You won't. It'll be the same. It's always the same. Don't you understand" — though she knew he did, and would have kissed him for his daring if it were possible — "I can never get close to anyone!" "Stories are never fixed." A spasm of disgust tightened his face; he had seen her again, fat and muscle cased around bone, beauty stripped to reveal the nonsensical repulsion that seized them all. But he did not look away, though he blanched with the effort, and when it passed he was still watching her. "It's one of their great virtues. They don't tell themselves: they are told, and change in the telling . . . Please, nameless woman, Adam's second helpmeet, I don't know what to call you and I don't know if I ever will, come see me again. When I've forgotten. When you can bear to see me." He added, broken-smiled, "At least we'll get another crack at that curry."

She could give him no promises. She did not know if she could ever learn to see him without the memory destroying her, if she could endure the same loss a second time, if she could bear to do such a thing to him; or whether between this moment and next summer she would meet someone else and be drawn to this new one as surely and fatally as to Adam Loukides, to enact the old pattern once again in pain. Across the road, the sun was settling a film of gold across the late cloud-trailed sky. Four or five children were playing in a yard; she tried not to see how casually, carelessly, they touched. Her mouth still remembered the particular flavor of Adam's kisses, her fingers knew the curl of his hair and the roughness of his jaw. Better to walk away, to keep walking, continuing the endless journey of story sealed onto life. But no one had ever asked her to come back. She had never waited to see if they would.

"All right," she said quietly. "When you've forgotten." What she would do then, she would have to wait and see. But it was enough now for Adam; and, perhaps, for her.

She left him as she had come to him, solitary, carrying nothing but the gathering weight of memory, her beauty and her immortality, and her despair. Walking away from Adam, she walked down the street that led away from his grandfather's apartment, going east. Her shadow splayed before her. She followed it, past the used book store and the Thai restaurant, over the scrubby green and the parking lot outside the library: moving nameless through the streets, lost in the world, and loved.

Three Young Men
By Romie Stott

A shape with lion body and the head of a man,
A gaze blank and pitiless as the sun,
Is moving its slow thighs, while all about it
Wind shadows of the indignant desert birds.
                    -W.B. Yeats, "The Second Coming"

This is what happens when you are burned alive - your capillaries expand and plasma leaks out of your blood. The hairs burn before the skin. If you can think, you think the leaking plasma is sweat, because plasma is clear like sweat. But sweat falls out of pores and the surface of your skin has charred - first on your legs and arms, then your torso, and finally your face.

As your blood vanishes, you dehydrate. Your heart races, then slows, then beats too fast for life. No matter how quickly it beats, there is not enough pressure to move your deflated blood; fluid pools in your ankles. The water left in your cells expands as it evaporates. Your intestines explode. Melting fat seeps from new fissures.

Your lungs and brain fill with unprocessed blood. Your lungs are still working, although you feel they are not.

When enough of your blood has boiled away, you suffocate.

I live in the home of a king who is not my father, who becomes a beast at night. I know this because my friend Daniel dreamed it. Then I and my brothers dreamed it also. We are not from this country. We were taken from our parents. The king calls us by names that aren't ours. Privately, we use our true names, but can no longer remember to whom each belongs. I believe I am Azariah. My brothers and I do not share parents, yet we are the only family we have. Daniel is different; he knows he is Daniel.

Since we came here, the priests have pretended to teach us magic. We spend long days crouched before gold statues, staring into bowls of water - sometimes gold, sometimes iron. We try to see the future in them. At dinner, Nebuchadnezzar the king asks whether we are happy and what we have learned. If he asks me directly, I say, "God is great." More often, he asks no one and everyone; I watch the faces of my brothers and hold their hands beneath the table. We know we aren't wizards - only hostages. And our teachers aren't more than men who throw silver and clay and guess what the patterns mean.

Maybe I am named Mishael.

One day, my brother who may be Hananiah whispered that we would never see anything in the bowls. "False gods give false sight," he said. "If Babylonian gods send us visions, it may be a trick to make us act against ourselves. By seeing their visions, we should be corrupted into worship of gold and iron and silver and clay. That's what the king is waiting for."

I knew he was right, for the only truth left is the truth we remember from outside, and we remember less and less. I took to my bed for the rest of the day, too lonely for fantasy work. No idol priest stopped me.

Late, late in the night, in the dark of no moon, my curly-haired brothers slipped under the covers. They pressed their faces to my shoulders, and I felt sweat or tears. "We have to hold together," my brothers said. "Outside these walls, we are princes. It may be that our sovereignty is gone, and our mothers and fathers pay tribute to Nebuchadnezzar, but things change with time. Our land was given to us by God, and God will return it. We are chosen. Though we forget our names and our temple, we must never forget God."

"The only land of God in this place is in us, and in Daniel," I said.

"Then let us look into each other," we agreed, "and wait for God to reveal himself."

We resolved to never again be separated, even for the smallest moment. The next day, without discussion, we sat at our seeing bowls and focused our thoughts on King Nebuchadnezzar, dreaming dreams to fill his head. Never again would we wait for revelations of gold and iron and silver and clay. Instead, we would project our own truth - God's truth - and overtake the king.

"What do you see?" asked our teachers. We kept our mouths serious, but our eyes laughed to each other. We prayed, and we were strong. We knew that soon we would dream the same dream, and Nebuchadnezzar would dream it with us, and we would know how to escape. That was real magic.

We never spoke to each other about what we saw when we watched the water; words would ruin us.

And so we knew surprise at dinner, when Nebuchadnezzar did not ask what we had learned, or whether we were happy; merely turned to Daniel and began to describe the nightmare. He had dreamed of a giant metal man carving stone from a mountain. The next night, the same dream - but the stone fell on the man, crushing him. The next night, the metal man lay with his gold head and iron feet beaten to dust. The next night was dreamless, and yet it was followed by a night of dream - the stone became a new mountain, growing to cover the earth.

The king began to drink heavily, to try to sleep while awake and slow the growing mountain. As the weeks passed, exhaustion and anger harried him. He executed his wise men for not curing him; but we knew we were safe. We were valuable hostages. We kept dreaming at Nebuchadnezzar, and waited for the court to fall apart like the nightmare's metal man.

After days and weeks of victory, Daniel told the king that his dream merely conveyed future history - not a nightmare, but a foretelling of movements of kingdoms, long after his lifetime. Nebuchadnezzar, who loved prophets, was so deeply flattered that he immediately welcomed sleep, and his nightmare. He gave Daniel fine clothes, a private room, and access to the palace.

The dream had escaped our dominion.

"Why did you do that?" we asked Daniel.

"I was frightened," he said.

"We were safe."

"His men were innocent."

Daniel had not known our implicit plan; we understood then that he was outside our mind. And yet we could only respect his interpretation. Until he spoke, we had not known what the symbols meant - only that they frightened us and terrified our jailer. Perhaps we had not sent the dream to Nebuchadnezzar; God had sent the dream to us, to reveal Daniel. We watch for God's next revelation. We abandoned our water visions to experiment with blistering herbs, rubbing them in small cuts and examining the pus that bubbled out. We studied the empty stars to fill up time.

After months of waiting, Nebuchadnezzar became tired again, drunk and sullen.

"My dream has changed," he told Daniel. "Now there is a healthy fruit tree on which countless animals feed, but the tree is cut down, and the stump is chained to the earth."

Daniel's answer was quick.

"It means the same as the last," he said. "You are the tree, and the animals which feed from it will extend your rule forever. Even after you die, your roots cannot be removed from the earth."

Nebuchadnezzar relaxed, and drank so much wine that he had to be carried to bed. Daniel smiled and laughed with him, but my brothers and I knew his mirth was false. Daniel doesn't laugh if he means it. He smiles.

He came to our room that night. He stood at the door, staring at us tangled up in our bed as we looked back at his silhouette. Eventually, he spoke.

"I lied about what the dream meant. It's dangerous. I haven't figured it all out yet, but I don't think we should eat the king's meat anymore. It's not safe."

Then he turned and left. We curled tighter around ourselves and closed our eyes. We had the second part of God's message, straight from Daniel. Act like a Babylonian, and you become a Babylonian. Eat a beast's food, and you become a beast.

When we woke, we were joyful. We ate nothing. Our friend the cook plied us with bread soaked in milk, but we batted it aside. Looking at the cook's face, and the splatter of milk, we felt our own power. We felt our strength to reject. Then we screamed in delight until it became too much, and we had to run from the kitchen.

We spent the day hiding in the garden, not speaking. Sporadically, one of us laughed; we had to move from bush to bush in case a gardener heard. This was the joke: Daniel was stronger than we were, full of self, but because he was strong, he was limited. Daniel understood, so Daniel appeased. We were weak. Our power barely extended to the tips of our noses. Therefore, we were nothing but children of God. We made poor livestock. And we would show Daniel escape in place of survival.

Three Young Men by Romie Stott

Nebuchadnezzar's dinner table was laden with feast foods; we were excited but not enticed. Daniel dutifully filled his plate with vegetables. We would risk no contamination. We shivered as our eyes ran over the piled-high platters, coated with stringy glazes and vivisected fruit, wilted, stuck-on stems of leaves, flesh that puckered at the smallest poke of a fork. We tried not to breathe in the smells - to fill our mouths with only empty air. We stared at our bare plates, and the festive atmosphere tapered into grim suspicion. Our dinner companions' conversation turned inevitably to our empty plates, which led to forced defenses of the food and the festival. The conversations became too awkward, then slowly died into noises of diligent knives and forceful chewing. On his great throne, Nebuchadnezzar gradually stiffened, and his face purpled. If someone in that room had been strong enough to be jolly, the moment might have broken, and passed on. But the tension was too high. No one dared to laugh or smile with the king's eyes looking down at them. Nebuchadnezzar scanned the room, angrier with each unsmiling mouth, seeking his reflection in our gleaming, unpolluted chargers.

"I insist you eat something," he said, his fleshy jaws vibrating. "You hurt cook's feelings horribly already. And I promised your parents I'd keep you safe."

"Werewolf," we said. "We name you before God."

One of us pushed a cooked ribcage to the floor.

Nebuchadnezzar didn't speak. He rose from his throne with his lips curled back. His arm reached slowly forward, fingers like claws. Everyone stopped breathing, and those who had eaten looked seasick and bloated.

"Pick that up and eat it," Nebuchadnezzar said. His voice was taut, then quiet. We had not expected such a grand confirmation.

"No!" we said, leaping from our seats.

"Cannibal!" we shouted.

As though all the lights and noise in the room had died, we saw just us, the table, and him. And Daniel, still seated, luminous but silent.

"I ask you again," said Nebuchadnezzar. "Eat. Anything." But we had found a way not to be trapped, and we were not giving up.

"Wolf! Wolf! Wolf!" we shouted.

The sound of the room came back, and Nebuchadnezzar walked away.

Guards led us to a cell with no light. We slept and woke several times. It may have been days. It may have been minutes. After a time, Daniel visited. He looked pale.

"This is not what I meant," he said. "You have to eat. The king will kill you before he lets you starve to death."

"He wants to fatten and eat us," we said. "That's what his dream meant. He is a wolf, and we are his cows. We can eat his food, or we can choke him with our bones."

"No," said Daniel.

"You'll see, Daniel. Watch him go mad, like an animal."

"No. But he is a proud man, and he will kill you if you do this. You must eat."

"No," we said. "We will not eat. God will protect us."

"Please," said Daniel. "The smallest apology, and you'll be forgiven. I know it. Just let the king save face." He looked miserable, but we weren't mad at him. Each day, he came and implored us; we waited until he left and then sang hymns of comfort.

"This is absurd," Daniel said. "You think I don't understand, but I do. This hunger strike doesn't mean anything to Nebuchadnezzar - or to God - only your ego."

"We are who we are," we said.

"Exactly," said Daniel. "That doesn't change. Make small adjustments that don't matter, and wait for your moment. Trust in the Word."

"We do trust," we said. "We are waiting."

Eventually, Nebuchadnezzar's chief judge showed his face.

"Do you insist on starving yourself, in defiance of the king and your parents?" he asked. We smiled at him in a way we hoped was friendly.

"We are not starving," we said, turning our bodies around so he could see our substance.

"Will you apologize before our gods?" asked the judge.

"You have no gods," we said.

Later, armed men entered the cell and bound our hands. They led us down corridors we'd never seen, to a hot stone room where Daniel waited, sweating. He held a ball of dough shaped like a ram.

"Please," he said. "It's safe. I made it." We shyly shook our heads.

"God," we whispered.

A metal door was set in the wall, and it opened on a room of flame, a furnace that heated the palace. Our guards hung back, but we stood straighter. Without prompting, we filed through the door, and it shut behind us. We looked back through the crack as it closed, and saw Daniel's awed face, lit by the fire that danced around us. With our clothes alight, we must have looked like angels.

Every night, the king sets out a feast, to show his power. If we don't eat, he is angry. He says he worries for our health, but this is a lie for his human face; beneath it, the beast face is laughing. We believe the poison is only in the meat, but we do not know. When we stopped eating, we were strong and impervious to pain. When we leapt, we could wait in the air before coming down.

The king thinks we will burn because he is a beast, and beasts burn. But we are made of clay. Fire can only harden us.

The Chronicle of Aliyat Son of Aliyat from the Chronicles of the Kings of Ashdod
by Alter Reiss

It was in the fifteenth year of the reign of Aliyat son of Aliyat son of Obedagon, of the line of Callioth, that a stranger came to the city of Ashdod, an exile from the kingdom of Judah in the hills.

The guards at the gate made a mockery of this man, for he was a stranger, and he wore a cloth over his face that none might see him. Then the stranger unhooked the cloth from one of his ears, that they might see the corner of his face.

When the guards saw the corner of his face, they could not speak, so great was their fear, and they fell down upon their faces.

Word of this was brought before the king, and he commanded that the stranger be brought before him. "Who are you, Judean," said the king, "that you come into the city with a cloth before your face, that none might see you, and before whom the guards at the gate have bowed in fright?"

"Hear me, O King of Ashdod," said the stranger, and he spoke in the old tongue of Ashdod. "Judah in the hills is like a stick that is rotten in its heart. They drove me forth, so I have given their king over to leprosy, and their people to the slaughter. I have come before you, Aliyat son of Aliyat, to offer you a precious gift, that will see your enemies driven before you, and will see the walls of your city rise up even to the heavens."

At this, the nobles who were in the court did scorn, saying. "Who is this that comes to the court of Ashdod, who speaks in the old tongue of Ashdod? Let him go back to Judah in the hills, where he can follow sheep with unshod feet, and drink young wine." And, indeed, the stranger's feet were unshod, and the fringes of his coat were covered in the dust of the road.

"Well that you mock, O children of Ashdod," said the stranger. "And well that you laugh, O sons of Callioth. Judah has laid waste to your lands, and built cities in it, even to the plain of Gaza. In the North, Assyria grows strong and proud, and her armories grow fat with arrows, which thirst for your blood. Well that you mock, and fine that you laugh."

But Aliyat son of Aliyat, of the line of Callioth did not laugh and did not mock.

"Show us, then," he said, "a proof of the gifts that you offer."

"Certainly, O King of Ashdod," said the stranger. "Have them bring before me a slave and a female slave."

The slaves were brought before him, and he extended a finger toward them, and the slaves were struck with leprosy, so that their faces became white with it, and they fell to the ground. "Thus I have done," said the stranger, "to Uzziah son of Amaziah, when I was cast from Judah of the hills. He who was a mighty king now sits outside the city, in a separate hall, and even the slaves of his people will not enter there, lest they be defiled by him. Thus shall I do to all the enemies of Ashdod, and to those who conspire against it."

The men of the court were amazed as they looked upon the male slave and the female slave that had been struck with leprosy, so that their faces had become white with it, and that they fell upon the ground, and the men of the court grew fearful.

"What would you have from us," said Aliyat son of Aliyat, "that you will do these things on our behalf?"

"Build for me a temple, fifty cubits in length by fifty cubits in width, with a roof of strong timbers, so that I may conduct the worship of my god, where none shall desecrate the rites of my god by gazing upon them."

The workers of Aliyat son of Aliyat built a temple for the stranger, of fine cut stone, fifty cubits in length, and fifty cubits in width. It was decorated on the outside with gold and precious jewels, and none but the stranger would enter the precincts of the temple. There were brought bullocks and great-bellied sows for sacrifices, and slaves and female slaves, and soon the stranger did as he had promised, and delivered gifts unto Aliyat son of Aliyat.

For a time, the stranger talked with the priests of Ashdod, bestowing upon them his lesser secrets. Many things he told them, which they had known and then forgotten, and which sorely troubled them. Gabridagon of no father, High Priest of Moloch, who conducted the dread rites of Moloch, and who guarded the secrets of Moloch's temple, spoke for a time with this stranger. When the stranger left the temple of Moloch, he was seized with a great fear, so that he fled the city of Ashdod and the lands of the Philistines, and he was never to again be seen in the lands of man.

When the stranger saw that his wisdom was scorned, the stranger gave to the people gifts. Gold and silver he gave, and fine old wine, and poppy juice for their delight. Male slaves and female slaves he gave, comely in form, who spoke not, and who worked tirelessly. Fine horses and fine cattle, powerful in their work, came to Ashdod, and the storehouses of grain were filled without the work of the harvestmen.

The gifts the stranger gave to the king of Ashdod were greater than horses, slaves and silver. The enemies of Aliyat son of Aliyat, among the nobles and among the priests, were stricken with plagues, or were seized by fits so they died, or were found on dry land with their bellies filled with water, as though they had drowned. Because the power of Ashdod grew heavy upon the land, Ashkelon bowed its neck to the king of Ashdod, and even the princes of Gaza sent him tribute.

As the gifts waxed and grew large, so too did the price. Animals of every sort were brought to the stranger's temple and slaves in their hundreds, to feed the hunger of his god. Smoke of his sacrifices did not rise to the sky. Not even the blood of offerings left his temple.

The Chronicle of Aliyat Son of Aliyat by Alter Reiss

In his youth, Aliyat had heard the voice of the people, but as his power grew, he heard not the voice of the people, or of the priests of the gods of Ashdod, or of the noble families of Ashdod. When an enemy of the king was killed, Aliyat would send the sons and the daughters of that man to the stranger, so that they would enter into the temple, and were never seen again.

In those days, the priest of Dagon in the high temple of Ashdod was named Melichibal son of Abedizevuv son of Amnon the Israelite. He was struck with a plague of the kidneys, and he died in the temple while making the morning offerings. The people were sorely afraid, for Melichibal was beloved, and he had spoken ill of the nameless priest of the hidden god.

Ishbal, son of Melichibal, tore his hair when he heard of the death of his father, and cut his flesh with a knife, but he did it in a secret place, so that none might know his grief, and he wore rich clothing with his sackcloth beneath.

"When the king hears that I do not mourn my father," said Ishbal in his heart, "he shall make me priest of Dagon in the high temple of Ashdod in my father's stead. And when the king comes to bring the royal offerings on the festival of the dying moon, I shall strike him with my mace of office, and he shall die. Thus shall the blood of my father be avenged." For Ishbal knew that his father's death came from the king.

And so it happened, that Aliyat son of Aliyat made Ishbal son of Melichibal priest in his father's stead, and when it came time for the festival of the dying moon, when Aliyat son of Aliyat brought his royal offerings, Ishbal son of Melichibal struck him with the mace of office, so that the blood flowed freely from the head of the king, and he died.

When they saw what Ishbal son of Melichibal had done, some of the mighty men of the king, who were his guard, pierced Ishbal with their swords in the thigh and in the breast, and Ishbal died upon the altar of Dagon. But the hearts of the multitude who were in the temple for the festival were not with the king, and they took up burning staves from the fire on the altar of Dagon, and they beat the mighty men of the king with them so that they died, and then they went out in the streets of Ashdod.

Many men had lost their fathers to the temple of the stranger who had been cast out of Judah, many had lost their sons, or their daughters, and had seen their land given to the stranger, so that they no longer loved the rule of Aliyat son of Aliyat. They cast down the stones of his palace to the foundations thereof, and they killed all the servants of his body, and all the officers of the court. Yanshuf his royal wife and Reuma his concubine, and also the sons of Aliyat they killed, so that the royal line of Calioth was utterly extinguished.

From the ruins of the palace, the people came to the temple of the stranger, into which he had fled, when he had heard the news of the death of the king.

The doors of the temple were crafted of brass, ten cubits in height, and bound up with iron. When the people came upon the gates of this temple, they did not know what to do, for the doors were too strong to force open.

Then Zarikash son of Balnatan, of the mighty men of the king, took up an axe, and hewed down a sycamore that had stood in the outer courtyard of the temple, and the people made it into a ram, to force open the gates of the temple.

The first time the ram touched the door, a voice came forth from within. "Hear, O people of Ashdod, and listen, sons of the Philistines. You have killed a king on this day, and spilled the blood of princes. Return to your houses, and repent your crimes, lest you assuredly be destroyed." And of the moment the ram first touched the door, the gold and the silver that the stranger had given turned to slime and decay.

The second time the ram touched the door, a voice came forth from within. "Hear, O people of Ashdod. And listen, sons of the Philistines. Baal will not protect you, and Dagon has turned his face from you. Ashtoreth hides in her weeping, and Zevuv has departed from your lands. Return to your houses, lest the last of the gods of this land depart from you." And of the moment the ram touched the door for the second time, the grain that the stranger had given turned to slime and decay in the storehouses.

The third time the ram touched the door, a voice came forth from within. "Hear O people of Ashdod,

45

and listen, sons of the Philistines. Judah grows proud in the hills, and Edom grows numerous in the desert. In the north, the armies of Assyria grow ever larger, and they lay in provisions for the conquest of your land. Only through strength will Ashdod stand, and if you strike at me, you lose a third portion of your strength." And on the moment the ram touched the door for the third time, the slaves and the female slaves, and the horses and cattle that the stranger had given turned to nameless, shapeless things, that tore and rended at the flesh of those who owned them.

The fourth time the ram touched the door, the doors burst open, and a spirit of corruption sprang from the temple. Many were struck dead by that spirit of corruption, and many others were sickened so that they never recovered. But still the people pushed forward, and would have entered the precincts of the temple, when a thing came forth, the like of which was never seen before, and the like of which should never be seen again.

The hidden god of the temple seemed to some like an octopus of the seas, and to others, like a great frog, but all who saw it knew it as an abomination, and they fled from it, or covered their faces so that they saw it not. All the men who had battered at the gates of the temple fled from the monster, except Zarikash, son of Balnatan, who took up his sword, and struck at the monster. It availed him not; when his sword struck the monster, his arm withered, and he was struck senseless where he stood.

The Chronicle of Aliyat Son of Aliyat by Alter Reiss

The temple of Dagon, the monster destroyed, and the temples of the Baalim, the abomination laid to waste. The trees of Ashtoreth were uprooted, the statues of the gods were humbled, and their servants were stricken with madness or slain. The gates of Ashdod opened like wounds, and the people fled the city like blood.

Stones cracked where the abomination that came from the temple stood, and the water beneath the earth recoiled. Finally, the mouth of the earth sighed, and a chasm opened up which swallowed the monster, and the temple, and the stranger who had been cast out from Judah in the hills, and many of the houses and the people of Ashdod.

Then the earth spoke, and it said, "Woe unto me that such a one is taken into my hidden depths," and there was a great earthquake, even unto Moab and the furthest borders of Egypt. Upon the altar of the stranger, ten thousand died, and from the earthquake, ten thousand myriads. And Athishuf son of Menelegar, who had been among the men who carried the ram at the temple gates, sang this song:

The towers of Ashdod are broken
The pride of Gaza is reduced.
The line of Calioth is extinguished
The crown of the Philistines is lost.

Woe unto us, the children of Dagon,
Let us grieve, who followed Calioth from the West.

47

Woe unto our sons, who will be sold as slaves,
Woe unto our daughters, who will be sold as female
slaves.

The towers of Jerusalem are broken
The pride of Samaria is reduced
Not one stone stands on another in Lachish,
Gezer is an utter ruin.

Who shall aid us, when the Assyrian comes?
Who shall protect us from the sword of the North?
Aram is conquered and Egypt is a pit of decay
And all of our strength has been lost.

When the monster was swallowed into the earth,
some of those who had been struck with diseases were
cured, and some of those who had been struck
senseless were again able to stand. None of those men
would ever speak of what they had seen when they lay
in stupor, but they were all seized with great fear when
they looked too long upon the waters of the sea, or
when they gazed upon the light of the stars.

Zarikash son of Balnatan ruled in Ashdod after
Aliyat son of Aliyat. The right arm of Zarikash was
palsied from the time that he struck the monster, and
he suffered from terrors. In the twentieth year of the
reign of Zarikash during that time of year when the
influence of the dog star is strongest, certain strange
fish were brought forth from the ocean. When he saw

these things, Zarikash threw himself from the highest place of his palace, and none could say why.

Baldad son of Zarikash of the line of Balnatan ruled in Ashdod for seven years. Then he was stricken with a fever of the blood, so that he died, and Athishuf son of Baldad of the line of Balnatan ruled in his place. In the thirty-second year of his reign, Athishuf son of Baldad was taken captive to Assyria, and he and all his line died in their exile beyond the Euphrates.

King David and the Spiders from Mars

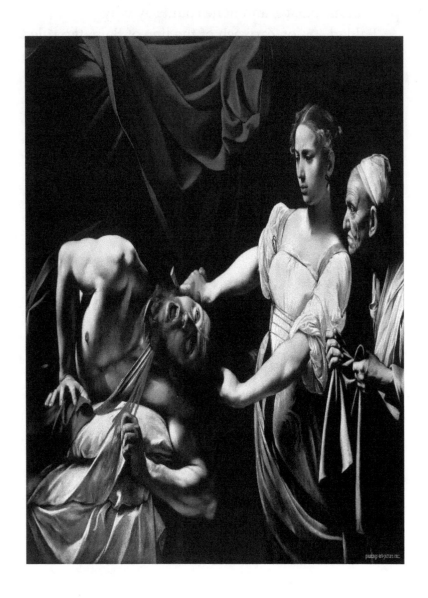

Good King David
By Jeff Chapman

Uzzah strode across the courtyard, angling for the double gate, the only break in the palisade. A predawn mist swirled at his ankles and a damp chill seeped through the woolen tunic beneath his leather brigandine. Two small fires crackled on either side of the path. Ash glowing red spiraled upward in the heat and smoke before burning out to black and disappearing in the night sky. A stench came forth from hell or the gates, metallic and musky like battle and blood but faint like a memory.

A shadow passed the gate. "Halt," shouted Uzzah. He gripped the hilt of his sword. "Who walks the King's ground without leave?"

"And who challenges the King's watchman?" the shadow answered.

"Ahio," said Uzzah. The brothers clapped each other on the shoulders and then stepped closer to one of the fires to warm their hands. "I expected to find you on the wall."

"I would be, but . . ."

Uzzah followed Ahio's gaze to a dark corner of the palisade blackened with shadows from the walkway overhead.

"There's something foul in the air tonight."

"Aye," said Ahio. "I came down to have a look."

They nodded to one another, drew their swords, and advanced toward the wall, following the sick scent.

"Who's there?" Ahio shouted in a tone backed with steel, a command rather than a question.

A groan answered them, a mournful, wavering note, reeking of festering wounds but very far away like the splash at the bottom of a well reverberating to the surface. The watchmen stopped their advance. That groan belonged to no mortal man or any animal they had ever slain. They held their position, fighting their instincts, forsaking a bolt for the safety of the fire because no soldier wants to be the first to flee. They waited, but whatever groaned spoke nothing more.

"Unfold yourself," said Ahio.

The mist at the base of the wall glowed yellow and swirled with streaks of red, growing taller until it reached the height of a man. The watchmen stepped backward, gaping at the spectre coalescing before them.

The translucent form - a tall man with a stout body and arms like a bear - hovered in the shadow of the wall. Clotted blood matted a yellow beard that trailed down his chest. His gray mail was torn across his shoulder. Another gash sagged above the opposite hip. Splotches of dried blood, the color of ochre, stained the tunic as if he had splashed through a river of it. No helm protected his head.

"It's Uriah," said Ahio.

"Uriah the Geat," said Uzzah.

Uriah the ghost turned his eyes to them. Once the deep blue of a glacier lake beneath a summer sun, his eyes now weighed with the leaden gray of a rolling sea on the verge of a storm. With a tired, hollow voice, it spoke.

"Send for Absalom."

Uzzah and Ahio exchanged nervous glances. "We should rouse Nathanael the Wise," whispered Uzzah. "He'll know the witchery at work here."

"I'll fetch him at once," said Ahio but the hollow voice stopped him.

"You believe the dead deaf? That I am a conjurer's trick? Do you not see the blood of my wounds? Shall I turn my head and show you my cleaved skull? How many curses have I lain on the hand wielding the ax that parted me from Bathsheba?"

"'Tis not right to speak with the dead," said Ahio.

"Nor is treachery and murder," said Uriah. "You honored me once. Will you not honor me after death? Fetch Absalom."

The watchmen backed away. "If Absalom will come," said Ahio. "We will bring him."

"I shall wait," said the ghost, whose shape faded and folded in on itself, leaving a pillar of white mist.

The watchmen abandoned their post, a terrible breach for which a rope and tree awaited, but the ghost had addled their thoughts, bending them.

They found Absalom in the great hall, wrapped in elk hide blankets, sprawled on a dais before the king's table. A wolfhound with shaggy white fur lay beside him, resting its head on its paws. The sweet scent of mead punctuated here and there with the stench of vomit wafting from the stone floor. Orange embers dying in the fire pit reflected in the black pools of the hound's eyes. Its nostrils quivered, ever vigilant. It followed the movements of the watchmen as they stepped over and around snoring bodies. It growled as they approached. They gave a wide berth to the beast. According to rumor, the hound was the maker of eunuchs. Uzzah knelt beside Absalom and nudged his shoulder until he stirred.

The prince squinted at them. "What? It's still night."

"We beg your forgiveness. But Uriah the Geat has come back. He demands to speak with you."

"Uriah? He's dead, you fools."

"He's come in spirit," whispered Uzzah. "He waits for you by the gate."

"In spirit?" Absalom raised his head and shoulders, leaning on his elbow, his linen shirt trimmed with silver threads at the collar and wrists. "What does Nathanael say of this?"

"We came directly to you," said Ahio as he knelt beside Uzzah. "It's Uriah. We saw the wounds."

Absalom threw off the blankets and wrapped a bear skin cloak around his shoulders. Jabbing a finger at the hound, he commanded it to stay. The hound watched Absalom follow Uzzah and Ahio the length of the hall and into the night, then turned its nose to the thigh bone just beyond its front paws.

Good King David by Jeff Chapman

The watchmen stopped at the fires beside the path and pointed to the swirling pillar of mist that glimmered white against the shadowed wall; a dagger of moonlight had stabbed the fog. Absalom combed his fingers through twisted curls of his raven locks, as the full moon chased the western horizon, a single white eye behind scudding, wispy clouds.

"A trick of the moon."

"Do the moon and the fog speak?" said Uzzah.

Absalom glared at Uzzah and for a moment the two watchmen believed he growled deep and low at the back of his throat, but the night had already played with their senses and they no longer trusted them.

Uzzah bowed his head. "Forgive me, sire. I swear it spoke to us."

"With enough mead and wine the moon might do anything."

"It took shape when we approached," said Ahio.

"You deserted your posts. Joab would do much worse than hang you." Absalom laughed at their ashen faces. "You still possess enough wits to fear Joab so you can't be too witless. Give me some water. If I'm to speak to a ghost I can't go with a parched throat."

Absalom drank from a gourd that Uzzah proffered, with his head flung back to catch the last drops.

"Did it say it was Uriah?"

"There was no need," said Ahio.

"Uriah," shouted Absalom. "I've come."

When the pillar said nothing, Absalom leaped across the fire pit and strode toward the swirling mist.

The same groan accompanied the transformation, the cry of an agonized prisoner chained to the floor of a dry well. A snap and a spark and the pillar churned like a cyclone, spawning a man of light and shadow.

"Uriah," said Absalom.

"What is left," said Uriah, "when all a man holds dear is slashed from him."

Absalom took a deep breath, swallowed hard, and reached for his absent hound. "To what.... I was...." He held the ghost's gaze as he fumbled for words. "You summoned me? Surely you want my father."

"Do you ask the Frisians for aid to fight the Frisians?"

"You were loyal," said Absalom. "My father did you no wrong. You were entombed with more honor than a king."

"Guilt. My honor was a salve for his guilt. How quickly he found a husband for my widow. There is a festering sore at the heart of your house; it spreads its poison through the branches, sickening the flesh with greed and lust."

"Lies and slander. Who sent you?"

"There are some agonies that even the grave cannot contain. Idiot. Your father, our king and master, coveted my joy, seduced her into adultery and sent me to my death."

"You're one of Baal's demons, an agent from a Jutish sorcerer sent to sow discord."

"There is no need to sow when corruption grows abundant."

"Am I to believe hearsay about your widow? Prove your charges. Show me the corruption, this pestilence spreading through my father's house."

"You have a sister, a much beloved sister."

"Tamar."

"You shall see."

The light faded to gray shadow and the shadow to night and the ghost was no more. Absalom stared at the darkness below the wall. He heard the footfalls of the watchmen approaching from behind. He ignored them.

"Prince Absalom," said Ahio. "Was it Uriah?"

"I don't know," said Absalom. "Something malevolent. When day breaks, send Nathanael to me."

***

King David sat in a throne carved from the bole of a massive oak. Reliefs of bears and wolves spiraled around the legs. Eagles and falcons supported the arms. Angels soared across the back accompanying a burning tree whose flames jutted above the top. The eyes of every angel and beast sparkled with inlaid garnets. The carved flames sparkled with amber and crimson rubies. The chair sat in the center of a dais on the bottom of the hexagonal tower built on a motte in the center of his fortress. Moat and forest and fields encircled the stronghold; David's kingdom stretched beyond the horizon in every direction.

King David and the Spiders from Mars

David tapped his fingers on the armrests. His youthful beauty was a memory locked behind a protruding stomach and soft muscles. He was waiting for Nathanael the Wise in the chair from which he heard counsel, and judged.

Years ago, when he was young and honest, he relished these meetings. Now, Nathanael bore only accusations. From outside the tower, guards pushed open the double doors. Nathanael marched to King David without bowing or pausing. His staff clicked on the stone floor.

"May the Lord of the eternal fire that burns but does not consume bless you and shower mercy on your soul."

"And may he bless you likewise," David answered; his sigh rattled through the halls inspiring smirks from all quarters. "Your messenger said you had a vision, most urgent."

"I did. But I am not the only one. I met with Absalom before the sun rose to talk of ghosts, the ghost of Uriah."

"Absalom? Uriah's ghost?"

"Perhaps the dead hate treachery."

The two men glared at one another, an old bear and an ancient wolverine. David raised his white knuckled fists as if he could hide his animosity. Finally, David motioned as if he could command the prophet.

"I heard a story the other day. I suspect the plaintiffs will come before you within a fortnight. A wealthy farmer pastures his flock of thirty ewes beside the fields of a poor farmer who owns but one. The poor man's ewe is marvelous, with long strands of wool and a shiny coat. The rich farmer covets her and when the poor farmer takes his grain to market, the rich farmer grabs the prized ewe from the poor man's barn."

"The rich man's entire herd should be given to the poor man," said David.

Nathanael nodded.

"An abomination. And if the rich man orders the poor man murdered on his way home to guarantee the ruse?"

"Why are you telling me this story?"

"Don't you know?"

David admired the way that Nathanael paused to acknowledge the silence that gripped the hall, even as his fingernails dug into his chair. David knew Nathanael's next words and yet the pause allowed for hope.

"You are the rich man. You have disgraced yourself," said Nathanael. "Turned an honest wife into a harlot. Prayed for snow to cover your thieving trail. Conspired to slay your servant. It is beyond belief that one with so much can go to such extremes to take so little."

David stared at Nathanael's feet. The man wore no boots.

"The Lord has not given me boots, therefore I do not need them," he would say.

"Did God tell you all this?"

"It pained Him to reveal so much wickedness; you are still a favored servant."

David sat down, covered his face in his hands, and bowed his head, waiting.

"What more?"

"Nothing."

David dropped his hands from his face. Sunlight shot through the the six high narrow windows and fell on Nathanael's cheek.

The old man did not blink.

"Many will suffer," said David, "because of my rashness."

"If you do not tend the fire in your own house, other houses burn."

King David massaged his temples, another headache coming on like a storm brewing over the sea, where clouds gather and billow and darken.

"Is there no penance?"

"No."

"And what of Uriah's ghost?"

"The ghost appeared near the gate and asked to speak with Absalom. He doesn't know what it wants."

"Is this ghost a harbinger of my sorrows?"

"Perhaps. The Lord does not explain His methods."

***

David awoke to his angel hovering above him. Bathsheba. So beautiful. Her braided hair hung over her shoulder. If only she were a dream that would burn up like fog in the morning sun, something to be consumed at night with no consequence through the day. Bathsheba was the most potent of wines. A sip brought eternal craving and indulgence an eternal hangover.

She giggled when her almond eyes met his. She caused more jealousy among his wives than any other. He could not give her up, nor did he wish to. He touched her cheek and she held his hand in place.

"I see you are feeling better," she said.

"An angel's touch may heal even the most grievous wounds." His fingertips trailed down her neck, across her breasts. Bathsheba pressed his hand to her belly.

"Do you feel him moving? It is a son. I can feel it. He kicks with the authority of a king."

"I doubt you not. It will be a son." David smiled at her, but his fingers trembled as they sometimes did on the eve of battle, when the killer angels gathered, and premonitions harassed him.

Sorrows will harass you.

"What's wrong?" she asked.

"Nothing." He raised himself and kissed her lips.

"Has Nathanael said anything about our child's future?"

"No," said David, too quickly. "And you mustn't ask him. The old man doesn't like to be pestered, especially by pretty girls."

Bathsheba laughed as she nuzzled David's chest.

"There is something you need to know," said David. "A rumor is spreading that Absalom spoke to Uriah's ghost."

"Is it true? Surely just a bit of gossip."

"Nathanael believes him."

"But why would he appear to Absalom?"

"A drunken man's delusions."

They kissed again.

Outside the curtained doorway, a woman cleared her throat.

"What?" shouted David.

Maachah parted the curtain and entered followed by Michal the Barren.

"Bathsheba is needed. Michal will attend you now," said Maachah.

"Needed?" said David. "She's pregnant. She should be resting."

"Embroidery is hardly laborious," said Maachah, "and we must all work to complete the new tapestries."

David fell back on the pillows, waved his hand at Bathsheba, dismissing her. She left with a bewitching smile, mixing innocence and lust.

Michal sat on the edge of David's bed. David looked away. She whispered in his ear. "Should I tell the gossips why I am barren?"

"You wouldn't dare."

"I've heard that Uriah's ghost is walking the bailey. How many have seen him now?"

"Three, I believe, claim the honor."

"Indeed. You are lucky only dead husbands come back to make trouble."

"You are referring to that sniveling weakling."

"He treated me as a wife, and never had I need to save his life."

"He did nothing. And he was never your husband."

***

Absalom waited outside the great longhouse watching the autumn sun fall behind the forest. The fingers of his left hand curled around a leather collar that restrained the hound. As David's retainers entered the longhouse, they dipped their heads to Absalom in respect; kept a wary eye on the dog. Each man wore a necklace of gold and silver to honor their service. Joab the general was among the crowd.

"Joab," said Absalom. "A word."

Joab nodded. His sunken eyes appraised and rejected Absalom's authority.

"As you wish," he said as if in jest.

Absalom motioned for Joab to follow. Despite his age, he stood tall. Even limping, he moved with the confidence of a much younger man. As the two men and dog sauntered to the rear of the longhouse, laughter and boasting echoed through the wattle.

"What happened to Uriah?"

"He died fighting before the gate of a Frisian fort. You could have asked this of anyone. That is no secret."

"Why was he engaged where the battle was most heated?"

"A brave warrior hears the battle and runs to it, as a snake pursues a mouse."

"I've heard you ordered him to lead the assault."

"He was brave. Warriors of his kind pursue the enemy." Joab said. "They don't hide behind a beast."

"You walk a treacherous line, Joab."

Joab didn't blink or look away. Nor did he say more. He simply turned to the south and left. Absalom watched the old warrior limp away. Scars layered his arms and legs, one atop another like branches stacked for a fire. Someday, he thought. Someday that man will call me master.

***

Amnon watched her from the king's table - Tamar pouring mead into cups of wood or gourds - whatever would hold drink. She followed her mother Maachah, and offered wine to the retainers and their women. A silver circlet bound auburn hair which cascaded over her shoulders, and past her waist. A girdle of leather and gold rings cinched her apron-skirt tight across her hips and breasts.

The men stole glances as she passed. Amnon knew he was not righteous to lust after a half-sister, but he did lust. When she came near, he covered her hand with his. Her green eyes rose and then averted. He knew she was blushing, even as shadows whelmed her face.

As the eldest son, Amnon sat next to the king on the crowded bench. Amnon favored his left hand and frequently jostled David for space. Bathsheba, the pregnant new wife, the usurper, sat on the other side of David. Amnon ignored his father and his father's whore as they shared a joke and sipped their wine.

Tamar crowded next to Maachah at the end of the table. His half-sister didn't look at him. The way she avoided his gaze confirmed her feelings.

"Amnon," shouted David. "Have you seen Absalom?"

"Outside. With his damnable beast. Hunting ghosts, I suspect."

David paused as if to ask more, but then Bathsheba said something funny and the pair laughed. They barely noticed the three musicians that gathered at the hearth, carrying lyre, pan-pipes and a tambourine as wide as a man's chest.

Three times the bard struck the rawhide stretched across the tambourine's frame. The thumps and jangle chased talk and laughter to the darkest recesses of the longhouse.

"The lay of our people," the bard announced with a practiced, sweeping flourish. "We humbly offer to our Lord on high and our king on earth."

The minstrels bowed and waited for David's assent.

"Sing," said David. "Sing to the Lord and His people, for it pleases Him."

The bard began slow and lugubrious. He sang of the great migration, the wandering through the black forest. He sang of the godly flame that burned without smoke, leaping from tree to tree, crackling and roaring, burning without consuming.

Amnon turned to Tamar, who watched the musicians with dull eyes and lips that neither smiled nor frowned. He leaned close to his father's ear. "Father, I'm not feeling well."

"What pains you? Your head?"

"And my stomach."

"Take some wine."

"I will. And send Tamar to me. Her singing will soothe my ills."

"Of course," said David.

Amnon walked behind the king's table and behind the tables. Tamar didn't acknowledge his passing, but she would not ignore her father's command.

***

Absalom walked around the palisade's perimeter, diligent and wary and desperate for the ghost. He needed guidance and the ghost had told him things bright and preternatural. The hound ran beside him, and when Absalom stopped to search the shadowy spirals along the wall, the dog sat on his haunches - its snout pointing at the gibbous moon. Clamor and music spilled from the great longhouse. The bard would sing the "Lay of the Long Journey" and possibly another.

No mists swirled. Nothing groaned. Crickets chirped without pause. Absalom plodded on through dirt and grass. The hound loped alongside him. If the ghost spoke truth and the living rumors were not idle, blood of treachery stained his father's hands. Such a man could not rule with trust and honor.

From the opposite side of the bailey, a sobbing wail brought Absalom and his hound to a stop. A lament sliced through the night, The dog stiffened. Her wails defied mending. Another ghost, he thought, another spirit to beguile.

Absalom saw her as she ran around the edge of a longhouse, and hesitated. The brooches were missing and her tattered shift slipped from her chest. A single brooch held at her right shoulder.

"Tamar," shouted Absalom. The girdle that had bound her waist was gone. Bruises striped her naked arm and shoulder. Tamar threw herself into Absalom's embrace, sobbing his name. He wrapped his bear-skin cape around her shoulders and held her until her sobs subsided.

"Who did this?"

New sobs drowned her speech.

"Tamar," he said.

"Amnon . . . He feigned sickness . . . Asked for wine. Father sent me."

From father to son, he thought, spreading its poison through the branches. Greed and lust. The ghost's words thumped his head, like an army beating their shields with swords.

"It was a trap," he said.

Tamar shook her head.

"Amnon is nothing to you. Come."

He led her to his house, tugging her arm, as he walked. He bid her to rest while he secured his sword belt and hefted a bearded ax.

"I'll leave the hound outside."

"Don't kill him," she said.

"I'm not going to Amnon."

***

Absalom carried his ax into the hall with the blade raised above his head. He strode between the tables and benches and loyal followers. He looked to neither side. The light from the hearth's flames danced in the rafters. The firelight glistened off the polished steel blade. Heads were lolling on the table beside toppled cups; few remarked him. The bard was singing the lay of Goliath. He stood in Absalom's path, turned to him in mid-phrase; still singing as his voice trailed behind his senses. Absalom plowed past, knocking the musician aside. The dropped tambourine jangled discordantly.

King David, drunk with mead and Bathsheba, slammed his fist into the table.

"Absalom!" he bellowed.

A blanket of bewildered shock spread over the hall. Only the snapping fire and retainers lost to drunk snoring refused silence. No one moved.

Absalom covered the distance in three quick strides, mounted the dais, and buried his ax in the oaken table. Bathsheba screamed.

"Tamar," he said and then stopped to breathe, like a messenger who has run for miles. The weight of the words fell out in gasps and sobs. "Tamar has been raped."

"No," cried Maachah. "No. Tamar. Where? Where is she?"

Absalom eyed David.

"Who has done this," said David. "Let him hang from a tree until the crows have picked his bones."

The sycophants banged their cups in support. Michal knelt beside Maachah, folding her in a comforting embrace.

"Amnon," said Absalom. "Your son bears the guilt."

Anger drained from David's face. The chorus of cups ceased. Maachah wailed unabated. Michal hid her smirk.

"You bring us bad tidings, Absalom. We must have proof. Who told you? Who are the witnesses?"

"I have Tamar's word. Her bruises and torn clothing speak for themselves. No one else. Do you think Amnon would violate his sister in the courtyard?"

"Joab." David's gaze never strayed from Absalom. "Fetch Amnon to the tower. You'll find him in his house."

The old warrior motioned two soldiers to join him and marched away.

"Maachah and Michal," said David. "Go see to Tamar. Where is the girl?"

"She's resting in my house. I'll have to call off the hound. He's watching the door."

"Then do so," said David. "And bring her to the tower."

***

King David sat in the oaken throne of the eternal fire, from where he dispensed judgments. Because the Lord favored his reign, he assumed his verdicts just and pleasing, but now his thoughts stumbled as a sailor lost in a rising tide ready to collapse and suck all below.

The first blush of a red dawn lit the narrow eastern windows. A weak shaft of light crept among the shadows of the ceiling joists. Amnon stood before the King. Maachah and Absalom flanked Tamar, who wore a black veil and Absalom's cloak. Amnon stared at his father. Tamar bent her head toward the floor. Joab lurked at the edge of the shadows.

"What say you?" said David to Amnon. "Does Tamar lie?"

"She was not as I expected to find her," said Amnon, as if a buyer at a market

Tamar whimpered. Absalom held his sister to his chest.

"You have shielded your intentions from us, Amnon. Did you violate her?"

"A broken gate cannot be violated."

"Where is Nathanael?" said Absalom.

"I am king and father," snapped David. "I don't need a prophet to pass judgment on my own children. The Lord loves all his children. Disciplines and forgives . . . His greatness derives from mercy, not wrath." His family stared at him. David paused to gather his thoughts, for the road was uncharted and overgrown with thorns.

"I have suffered the sting of His anger," said David, "and savored the sweetness of His grace. No one knows the depths of His patience. Amnon, if she will have you, you shall marry Tamar and you shall praise her honor to all who will listen."

"No," shouted Absalom.

"I have judged and he will abide. A wise judge seeks healing and punishment, for the past and future."

"If the King won't defend his daughter, I will."

"It is done, Absalom," said Tamar.

"And if the holmgang speaks in my favor?" Absalom asked.

"Absalom, you confound me." David stood, his face crimson. "The matter is settled. The king's word is final."

"It is my challenge," said Absalom. "My right and duty."

David pressed his throbbing head between his palms. Blood law tied his hands. "The judgment," he said, "will honor the outcome."

"We'll spread the hide tomorrow," said Absalom, and ushered his sister and mother out the door.

"Joab," said David. "Take Amnon to his house and keep him there until the holmgang."

"Am I a prisoner?"

"I should have you executed. If not...." David held his tongue. "Leave me."

Joab led David's son away. The King held his aching head as the dawn greeted the walls with rouge.

***

Joab stood inside the door of Amnon's house.

"Absalom will kill you."

"Let him try."

"You are not afraid?"

"Is there purpose in your warning or idle rambling?"

Joab stared hard at Amnon as he scratched his beard. "Absalom has become a nuisance. A house can't tolerate wayward timber."

"Many speak ill of my father, the King."

"Absalom may do more than talk."

"And he doesn't like you very much, does he?"

"I serve David's interests."

"You want me to kill him. But I'll have to kill him anyway to save my own life. This is your doing, isn't it?"

"A victor strikes an enemy before he's ready. Your father doesn't have the heart."

"What's your plan?"

"I can smear a poison on the blade of your ax. A nick will kill him."

"And you will protect me."

"Who will avenge him? He's asking for a combat to the death."

"Rightly so," said Amnon. "And you're an old fool. If Absalom falls dead from a scratch, the King will note it. Everyone will know I poisoned him. I'll hang, but you'll get what you want. Very clever, Joab."

"I misjudged you."

"You're vulnerable now, Joab. I'll remember."

Joab turned to the door and then stopped. "Why is it you will not take Tamar? Even an old man can see her charms."

"The sight of her burns my eyes."

***

David sat in the oaken throne, listening to Joab. With every word, something wicked was growing inside his house, inside his kingdom.

"He stands outside the gate with his dog," said Joab. "I've seen him myself."

David sighed. "Go on."

"He stands before the gate and stops everyone. 'There is no king on the throne,' he tells them. 'There is no just man there to hear your pleas.' It is treason."

"It is an angry young man. He does not know the world. Mayhap he has truly spoken to Uriah's ghost."

"You must punish Absalom, publicly. His transgressions cannot be ignored."

"If his mind is addled, the holmgang will sober him. I've been thinking to honor Uriah."

As David spoke, one of the double doors swung open. Uzzah stepped past Joab and dropped to one knee.

"Forgive me, my king, but I bear wretched tidings. It is Bathsheba."

David leapt to his feet.

"What? What? What has happened?"

"Absalom," said Joab. "Coming to claim your wives."

"He'll suffer the cold steel if he's laid a hand on her."

"No, no," said Uzzah. "She has miscarried."

Sorrows will harass you; bring your kingdom to the point of breaking.

"It is the Lord's doing," he said. He stared past Joab and Uzzah with glassy, vacant eyes. "In the course of a day, I have lost three sons and one will never come home."

The King stood and walked between Uzzah and Joab. The doors opened when he shouted a command. He left the confines of the tower for the bright sunshine of the gate. Joab and Uzzah followed. David stopped before one of the fire pits where he could see Absalom standing with his hound, accosting all who passed. David knelt, scooped charred wood and gray ashes into his cupped hands. Ash sifted through his fingers, forming a gray cloud in the breeze. David, the King, raised his hands and poured sorrow over his head.

***

Absalom could not sleep. Tamar rested in his bed, curled atop an elk hide blanket. Their mother sat with her, stroking Tamar's auburn hair, as she had done years ago.

"What if I am with child?" Tamar asked. "It will have no father."

Maachah looked to Absalom. Words failed her.

"Father has lost his mind. A union with Amnon would be an abomination."

He left Maachah and Tamar and walked the palisade's perimeter with his hound, as he had done the night before.

"Uriah," he shouted.

The guards on the wall stared down at him. Some shared his doubts. Others found his shouts more frightening than any ghost. The guards talked of the coming holmgang. Had Joab's warriors not guarded Amnon's house, he would have hastened there to snap his brother's neck and cast the body into a food trough for crows and dogs.

Absalom neared the turning where the ghost had first appeared, his footfalls thudding in the trampled dirt; the dog padded beside him. The moon lighted a path darkened by shadows.

"Uriah," he cried. "Have you no more honor than the king?"

The hound stiffened and growled. Absalom scanned the darkness.

"Uriah?"

"Absalom." The voice was a woman's, soft and soothing.

Absalom furrowed his brows. "Who's there?"

Michal stepped from the shadows. Her face glowed white in the moonlight, framed by her black hair. Her lapis-blue shift seemed to float.

"Michal?"

"Call back your dog," she said.

He told the hound to sit, but it ignored him, until Absalom pushed down on its back, settling the hound on its haunches. It snarled at the darkest point of the turning.

"You are seeking a ghost," she said.

"The spirit knows the future," said Absalom.

Michal stepped closer, her scented oils wrapping him in a sweet cocoon. "I seek the future as well, but I am searching for the new king."

"The new king?"

"In the land of the living. David no longer rules. He clings to power like an oak holds its dead leaves. A wind is coming, Absalom. Does David defend his daughter? His servants?"

"No."

"Someone must be that wind that tears the power from his hands. What will you do?"

"King David has many friends."

"Do you know why I am barren? He fears a grandchild of Saul, so he locks me in an empty bed, wasting away with my passions."

"That is indeed cruel."

"And cowardly. Take the king's wife, Absalom. Lay with me."

He lifted her and kissed her and took her near the wall where they tumbled into the shadows, a jumble of arms, legs, and torn clothing. Michal made no effort to hide her joy. The guards heard.

The hound growled at the dark, giving no attention to the lovers. Laughter, faint and far, echoed in the shadows. A gust of wind whipped dead leaves into a spiral. Then they were gone - the laughter and the wind; only the hound had heard them.

***

Beneath the tower, holmgangs began at midday, when the sun would not favor either man. Short stakes secured the corners of an ox hide. Four hazel staves marked the outer boundary, the line of forfeiture.

David sat below the tower doors. A fresh layer of ash dulled his black hair's luster.

Men, women and children crowded around the three remaining sides. Some sat on the walkway that edged the palisade, their legs dangling over the side. Everyone who could come came. One of the fighters might be king some day and the other would die, bleeding on ox hide. Wagers and gossip and silence affirmed the holmgang's sacred truth.

Absalom held his war ax. Three wooden shields with iron bands had been arranged just outside the line of forfeiture.

"Where's Tamar?" Absalom asked his mother.

"Resting," said Maachah. "She wouldn't come. Said she couldn't watch you die."

"I'm not the one dying." Absalom looked across the hide. Amnon stood with war ax and three shields. "The Lord will punish the wicked, mother. I have faith in his justice."

Amnon's mother whispered in her son's ear. Michal stood behind her and smiled when her eyes met Absalom's. Absalom looked at his shields, ordered and equidistant. Until last night he was beyond reproach. The ghost said there is a festering sore at the heart of your house, spreading its poison through the branches. He was a branch as surely as Amnon.

The hound barked and lurched toward the hide. Absalom slapped Uzzah. "Hold him firm I told you."

Uzzah's face reddened as he tugged the hound back to a sitting position.

"Yes," he said through clenched teeth. The strain compressed his voice to a whisper.

David rose and stepped forward onto the hide. He looked from Absalom to Amnon. "It is custom that demands I ask you if your differences cannot be resolved without combat."

They shook their heads.

"And a father's love demands I ask again."

Silence greeted David.

"So be it. I vest Joab the authority to judge. May the Lord guide the righteous weapon. Absalom, your terms."

Absalom answered without hesitation. "Until death or forfeiture."

Shock rippled through the crowd.

"I expected as much. Joab, their contest is yours."

David eyed each young man before making his way back to his bench. Does he know about Michal, wondered Absalom. David usually knows all, but who would tell him?

"Arm yourselves," said Joab.

Absalom donned a helm with a chainmail curtain. He fitted a round shield to his forearm and took up his battle ax. Across the hide, Amnon did the same, but held his ax in his left hand.

At a signal, they crossed the boundary, stepped to the hide, and thumped shields. They leapt back as the shields clacked to give the impact a hollow sound. As the challenged, Amnon had the right of first strike. Amnon charged. Absalom blocked. Amnon attacked with a flurry of swings; each stroke drove his brother back. Absalom had little experience against a left-handed foe. He twisted out of position to block Amnon. As he neared the line of forfeiture, Absalom lunged forward, swinging low. He sliced Amnon's thigh. Amnon retreated. Blood stained his leggings and dripped down to his boots.

They moved about the hide exchanging blows. Uzzah exercised all his strength to hold the hound, who rallied whenever Amnon swung. David watched the contest. He didn't twitch or lean forward. Only when someone stepped near the line of forfeiture did he look to Joab for a signal, but none came.

When Absalom's shield splintered into three pieces, Joab called a halt.

Absalom and Amnon gulped water from gourds, as they fitted new shields to their forearms.

"Have you had enough, brother?" shouted Amnon.

Absalom eyed his foe for only a moment.

"Surely we have seen enough," said David.

The King's suggestion startled the crowd and set them to murmuring.

"The terms cannot be altered," said Joab. "You know that well. It is the ancient way."

"The Ancient Days did not make laws for us to fall upon as a vanquished captain falls on his sword." David studied the faces of his people. Implacable, they stared back as one, branches from a single bole waiting for affirmation.

Where was Nathanael?

Walking in the woods, no doubt.

He should have consulted Nathanael.

David brushed ash from his cheeks.

"Let it continue," he said.

Joab looked square at Uzzah and nodded. Absalom and Amnon stepped onto the hide. Joab raised his right hand, and when he swung it down, their shields crashed together. The crowd hushed as the pair attacked with new ferocity, driving one another over the hide. Thuds and grunts punctuated the fight.

Amnon landed a blow square on Absalom's shield. The shield deflected none of the hit's force and Absalom suffered its full weight and stumbled, catching his heel on one of the short stakes. He fell backward as his legs shot forward. He fought the instinct to spread his arms for balance, keeping his shield in front of his chest. Wind burst from his lungs. When he struck the earth, his helm bounced from his head.

David turned his head. Maachah screamed. Amnon raised his ax high, ready, when Uzzah let go of Absalom's dog. The hound leapt, crashing into Amnon as he swung. The ax wheeled through the air. The hound lunged for Amnon's throat, but Amnon struck first with his shield, knocking the beast away. It yelped as Amnon sank his ax into its chest. The hound's dark eyes rolled backward.

If he had time to think, Amnon would have relished killing the beast. He sat up on his knees, looking down at the dog, his ax dripping blood, his arm tensed to strike again. The crowd booed. Some shouted foul.

Absalom's dog.

Absalom.

As Amnon scrambled to stand, he caught a glimpse of his mother, her face crinkled in an anguished scream. Why should she scream, he thought. The beast is dead and Absalom has fallen. One more killing blow to mix the blood of master and servant, he thought as Absalom's blade cleaved his helm and wedged deep into bone and brain. Absalom could not remove it. He let loose of the handle. Blood rained down Amnon's face, his puzzled eyes on his mother. Amnon's body fell across the hound. The handle of Absalom's ax pointed to the tower.

Absalom looked to Joab. The old warrior nodded. He looked to the King, who stood at the edge of the hide. The King moved his mouth but no words came. He breathed deeply and tried again.

"The holmgang has spoken," he said.

Angry shouts rose from Amnon's supporters.

Joab held up his hand and the people fell still.

"The Lord has spoken," said David. "He has meted out his justice. Let this be an end to it."

***

David sat on the throne of the eternal fire. His elbows rested on his knees. Hunched forward he no longer filled the throne. His tunic hung loose and torn from his chest. Ash stained his face and arms, his leggings and boots.

Absalom faced his father, his clothes intact and free of ash. Amnon's body lay between them.

"Has justice been done?" said David.

"Holmgang has spoken the Lord's will."

"Did we truly hear what was said?"

"The crime has been punished. Something you wouldn't do."

"When I was young I saw justice as a staff, stiff and certain to lean on. Now it is like smoke. I see it and smell it and feel it. I know what it is, but I cannot hold it. We are fallible, Absalom. Fallen. We shoot our arrows through the mists as we face the sunrise."

"You've strayed from the path into the bog. That's what Nathanael will tell you."

"Do you speak for prophets now?"

Absalom did not answer.

"And how will you punish your own crime when you are king?"

"My crime?"

"Did you think you could fornicate with Michal in the bailey in private? Your ancient path ends in a tree, Absalom."

"Michal tells me she is wife in name only, that the king neglects her. Do you care so much for your castoff?"

"I thought you adhered to the law. Michal is a dangerous woman. She metes out great love and equal hatred. I've felt both. She betrayed her father once. She has betrayed me, and she will betray you."

"I've given her no cause."

David sighed. The Frisians surrendered land with far less effort. "To punish as the Lord is easy, but to show his mercy requires discipline and wisdom. A great king can emulate his master with both hands. Weakness, Absalom, favors only one."

"The ghost spoke of a festering sore at the heart of your house. I rebuked him, but I see now that he spoke true."

"Was it Uriah?"

"Maybe."

"And what did this ghost predict?"

"Tamar's troubles."

"And?"

"The ghost hasn't shown itself again."

"You should not seek counsel from the dead; certainly not the vengeful dead."

"I find the dead more honest."

"You should fear the one with nothing to lose."

"He wants vengeance on you, father. Not me."

"You seek counsel from a ghost who desires my ruin," said David.

Shouting outside the tower doors ended their talk. The doors burst open. Joab entered carrying Tamar's body. Her auburn hair, dark and wet, hung past his knees. A garland of flowers, white and red and purple, encircled her neck. Maachah followed, clinging to Michal. Water darkened their skirts.

"We found her beneath the ancient willow," said Michal, "submerged in the brook."

Absalom rushed at Joab and snatched his sister's body. Joab released his burden without a struggle.

"No." David stood, his cry echoing off the stone walls. "No, no, no." His voice trailed off as he collapsed, hid his face in his hands, and wept. Many will suffer. Those eyes might cost a thousand lives. Absalom laid Tamar's body at the foot of the throne. No one spoke.

"You sniveling old man," said Absalom. "What have you done? Speak it, so your days as king may end."

"Do not speak treason, Absalom." Joab drew his sword.

"Do you serve the people or an old man?"

"A king serves and leads his people. I am King David's hound."

Absalom looked at his father, at the ginger-haired head with a bald spot spreading from its crown. "

"You are finished," he said.

He dashed past his mother and Michal, out the open tower doors.

"Joab," said David. "Fetch him back. Bring my son back to me."

***

Joab crept along a path in the woods; an ash spear doubled as his walking stick. As he neared the brook, he heard cursing, Absalom's cursing. He stepped from behind a blackberry bramble. The brook slowed and widened near an ancient willow that Joab knew well. As a boy, Joab had climbed this tree and dreamed of warfare.

Inside the weeping leaves, Absalom cursed and lamented his dead sister. Joab almost pitied the boy. Absalom and his men were soft, easily trapped. Joab's boots splashed only twice as he crossed the brook and stopped at the willow's shade. Absalom's back rested against a branch. His leg twisted where his foot had lodged in the crook of two branches. Absalom laughed as he saw the old warrior.

"Joab! An old man has sent another old man to fetch me."

"That was the king's wish."

"The king," Absalom laughed. "You'll do whatever he asks."

"I loyally serve."

"And if there is a new king?"

"It will depend upon his worth. A king demands service. He does not beg for it."

"Then get me out of this tree."

Joab hefted his spear. Absalom had only a second to lose his smirk to fear.

***

David perched on the edge of his throne. Carved flames of orange and red amber and rubies normally shielded from view shone behind him. Three shrouded bodies lay on the floor. Dark red stains bloomed over the white linen. Narrow shafts of light filtered through the west windows and crawled high on the eastern walls.

Nathanael and Joab stood in the hall.

"He resisted," said Joab.

"You have been steadfastly loyal to me, Joab. But this . . ." He gestured at the bodies. Then he turned to Nathanel. "Have we come to the end?"

The old prophet shook his head.

"Your sighs will harry you; every night you will drench your bed with tears."

The Sons of Zeruiah
by Megan Arkenberg

Well, Mother, is this the story you wanted to hear?

It begins with my brothers arguing - arguing like starving tigers - Asahel flat on his back at the edge of camp, dust in his glossy black curls. Abishai straddles him, white hands closing around his throat, blood from his split lip staining Abi's lace cuffs. The old accusations cloud the air - like gunpowder, like cannon smoke, like the din of carrion birds and the moist stench of rot.

"Ungrateful fledgling," Abishai growls. "Your impatience will ruin us!"

"Please, Abi, I haven't eaten in months!"

"I haven't eaten in years!"

Not since father died. The familiar chorus rises in my throat. I bow my head over my musket barrel, polishing the grimy steel. Maybe this time I will be left out of it.

"Joab!" Abishai barks my name, and I rise trembling. Rise and go to him, where he chokes our younger brother in the dust. I wrap my arms around Abishai's chest and feel his heartbeat shudder through me, rapid as galloping horses.

"Let him go, Abi."

"This puppy doesn't know what he owes me," Abishai murmurs. "But you do, Joab, don't you? You understand the meaning of gratitude."

He loosens his grip on Asahel's throat, tips his head back against my shoulder. I kiss him dutifully, tasting blood.

It begins on the battlefield, with the huge black man in the forest green of Ish-Bosheth's commanders. Abner, son of Ner. We crouch behind barricade, and I feel Abishai's cold breath on my ear.

"Imagine how sweet his lungs must taste," my elder brother whispers, his eyes twin flames of absinthe green. "Imagine how they would feel bursting between your teeth."

And I imagine it. Oh god, I imagine it, and I leap on the enemy soldiers like a starving thing, ripping through uniform coats and waistcoats of green velvet, prying open ribcages with my bare fingers. Blood splashes across my face. I lick it away with a moan.

It begins with the chase, as Asahel bounds across the field after Abner, slipping in the battle-red mud. He flings off his rifle, his saber, his blue coat, and runs with a naked bayonet in his hand. Abner is panting, aiming a flintlock pistol behind him with shaking hands. His shot goes wide.

Asahel slips. Abner takes the bayonet from his hands.

It begins as he slits my brother's throat.

It begins with Abishai howling like a wounded wolf.

In all these ways, mother, it begins - this story of ours. And I am here again, at the beginning, as Abishai hooks his fingers under Asahel's bloody shirt. The white cloth tears easily. Then comes skin, deep brown from the sun, and hard muscle. Then the white barricade of ribs.

"If we don't do it, he's lost," Abishai says. "Gone to the crows and the dogs and the worms. Wouldn't he rather feed us, Joab? Wouldn't you, if you were dead?"

Asahel's blood smells sweet, far sweeter than a man's, but it is the sweetness of rot. I close my eyes. Abishai presses something to my mouth, something soft and hot and sweet like honey. I part my lips and feel the smooth tenderness of Asahel's lung.

Tears run into my open mouth. Their salt flavors the blood.

***

Two years later, Abner appears in David's court. Who brought him here? Abishai, somehow spreading a fever of politics in Ish-Bosheth's court, stirring up scandal with the fiery Rizpah. For two years I have kept my head down, my sword drawn, waiting patiently like a good soldier. Now I lift my head and he is gleaming black in the candlelight, resplendent in David's royal blue.

Blood thunders in my ears. Unthinkingly, I reach for the dagger at my belt. Abishai's icy fingers stop me.

"Not now," he whispers. "Let him celebrate his promotion, down in the city. Let him get lost."

A crowd of princes and nobles, courtesans and sycophants closes around Abner, and I breathe deeply.

Abishai presses a cold kiss to the back of my neck, and I follow him, a good soldier.

It begins down in the city, in the tangle of taverns and brothels that is the soldiers' kingdom. The mighty Abner stumbles through it. Pretty youths and rambunctious whores flicker around him, transposable, none lingering more than a moment. I take my place among them and embrace my brother's killer like an old friend.

He stinks from cheap wine and vomit and perfume. His unfocused eyes examine my face with no sign of recognition. Somewhere nearby, a whore with blue beads in her hair breaks out a bawdy song. Like a good soldier, I join in.

Abner's rough hands are scraping against mine, as though some animal part of his brain knows what I am about to do. My knife is too quick for this drunk, pleasure-sated beast. I thrust it deep into his abdomen, and his falling flesh drives it into his heart.

Blood sprays, hot and sweet. Blood sprays across my face and chest. I lick it from my lips, feel the heat of it soaking through my shirt, sinking down to my skin. My hands are slippery with it.

It begins with the whore's song faltering as she starts to scream.

***

The King's Guard comes to bring me before David. I let them rinse the blood from my skin and strip away my stained uniform. I hear rather than feel the manacles close around my wrists.

David's chamber is dead silent. The king sits on his gilded throne - Queen Abigail, Princess Michal and Lady Abinoam occupying three low chairs beside him. Grim-faced soldiers are liningline the walls like disgusted statuary. Someone pushes me to my knees. I glance back involuntarily, and see Abishai's cold placid face.

"Sons of Zeruiah," David says softly, "what have I to do with you?"

Another familiar chorus, mother. Are you proud?

It begins with David's declaration: "We will put on mourning for Abner. You yourself, Joab, will help bear his casket." And I bow until my forehead touches the floor. Obedient and humble, like a good soldier when everything goes according to plan.

It begins the day of Abner's funeral, when the day dawns wet, gray as mold. Abishai whistles cheerfully as he dons his uniform black. Like a captive lion, he is dangerous when he is hungry, but more dangerous when the feeding approaches.

He flings himself down on my cot, his red hair fanning across the pillow like blood in an alley puddle.

"Be sure you are left alone in the tomb," he says.

"I'll remember."

"Be sure, Joab."

I kiss him dutifully. His rough tongue tastes of starvation.

It dances with the weight of the casket, the damp wood digging into my shoulder, but I am too apprehensive to feel pain. The funeral procession winds through the tangled streets of Hebron and its audience of soldiers and youths and whores.

I watch for the woman with blue beads in her hair, but I do not find her.

It begins with the seven of us standing in the sepulcher - the casket bearers and I and the king, dressed in soft sables. David makes a speech that none of us hear. I lower my head and let my shoulders sag, as if burdened with guilt. When the others file out, I stay behind, kneeling on the cool marble floor.

David's eyes slide across me. I hear his lips part, but he says nothing. His mouth snaps shut.

When they are gone, all of them gone and the cold iron door clangs behind them I heave the lid from the sarcophagus. It bears Abner's likeness in copper, massive and impeccably beautiful. And there is the true Abner within, foul and bloody and rotting. I do not tear his clothes away like a lover, but like a ravisher, opening his body with brutal, bloodthirsty hands.

It begins back at the barracks, where Abishai has fallen asleep on my cot. Nearby, the other soldiers snore in the darkness. I press a lobe of Abner's liver against Abishai's lips, planting biting kisses on his neck and shoulders until he awakes.

"Joab . . ."

I silence him with another scrap of flesh. His tongue scraps against my fingers, sucking away the blood. Something snaps in him, in both of us, and we are tearing and biting and scratching, holding our breath so we won't be heard, hardly knowing whose skin breaks beneath our teeth, whose blood makes our bodies slippery. I cry out once, in pain or pleasure or both, and it is Abishai's turn to silence me, pressing my face into the sheets.

In the morning, Abishai is gone, and my cot is drenched in blood.

This is how it begins, mother. The story of your sons, the story of the time we loved each other. Or perhaps it is only a story about hunger.

A story is a knot. As the knot tightens, we strangle.

***

Years pass, and the knot tightens. Abishai and I ride at the head of the caravan leaving Jerusalem; Absalom is burning the city behind us. The sky glows orange, and crimson, and gold as honey. Behind us, David bows his head, and the firelight catches the silver streaks in his blood red hair. Bathsheba rides beside him. The court calls her the Black Queen, because she still wears mourning for her dead son, because she is a sister to shadows and deep water and night, because they are frightened of her. She wears a three-cornered military hat cocked over her cruel beautiful face, a pistol at her side, a string of royal blue beads in her coal-brown hair.

"So which of them is it?" Abishai asks, as if this were a pleasure jaunt, as though the king just out of earshot were not fleeing for his life. "The king or the queen? Which one has caught your attention?"

I shake the question off. The wind stings my face, stinking of ash.

"The one who was bloodthirsty enough to murder Uriah," Abishai muses. "That must be it, the scent you caught on the breeze. I've seen you watching them, little brother. You're hunting something. But which one?"

Abner has changed us—taught us strategy, and cunning, and ambition. Or perhaps they had been with us all along, and it was only Abner's flesh in my flesh, his blood in my blood that taught me to see.

"Shall I tell you a secret, little brother?" Abishai leans closer, narrowing the gap between us until our thighs touch and our horses fight for legroom. "I have a gift for you. A little something to spurn your hunt."

I feel gratitude like a cord around my throat.

"And what is this gift?"

Abishai glances at the burning city behind us, and winks, and the knot tightens.

The knot tightens as the road runs by Bahurim. The fields to our right and our left are pale with dust. Skeletal families watch us from the shadows of unpainted houses and slack-roofed barns. A farmer comes running at us with small rocks in his hands.

"You are being paid for the blood you spilled in Saul's kingdom!" the man shouts, lobbing the stones at David. The king does not even shield his face. "Usurper, murderer, justly you are overthrown by your own son! I curse you, I and all from Saul's kingdom!"

I draw my sword. Bathsheba raises her pistol at the same time. Abishai watches, his gun drawn.

"Let him be," the king commands. His voice sags with weariness, almost too quiet to hear. I return my sword to its sheath; Bathsheba moves her finger from the trigger. Green fire is burning in Abishai's eyes as he watches the mad farmer and the spittle flying from his lips, the wiry muscles bunching in his limbs. The knot tightens.

"Sons of Zeruiah, what has this to do with you?" David barks. He covers his eyes with a trembling hand. I take Abishai's arm. Bathsheba raises her pistol. Her eyes meet Abishai's and I shudder.

They hold the same green fire.

In the wood of Ephraim, David leads us on foot through the wet green shadows and the sticky sweetness of pine. Here in the dark and the damp, this is where we will make our stand against Absalom. My hair catches on a low-hanging branch. As I reach up to free it, Abishai catches my wrist.

"Don't fail me, Joab."

"Have I failed you ever?" I whisper, though the other soldiers have moved on, out of earshot. "When will you trust me, brother?"

He slaps me. My split lip does not begin to sting until he kisses it, tonguing the ragged edges.

Bathsheba is waiting for us at the border of the forest. She does not say a word, but looks toward the horizon, where Absalom's army masses in a sea of bloody red.

Abishai's cold fingers stroke my hair, and the knot tightens as they close into a fist.

***

We fan out through the forest, our dark coats melting us into the shadows, the stink of our powder masked by pine and rotting needles. I see a brief flash of red. But it is not a uniform – it is only Abishai's hair, his dark hat knocked aside by a branch. We creep low the ground, waiting, and the knot tightens.

Absalom's army rides into the forest. It is easy at first, pathetically easy, to shoot the poor horses out from under them, to pick off the prone riders with knives and bayonets. Blood sours the air. The screams are swallowed by gloom. Between the clutching branches, the sun is a red ball of shot in the steel-gray sky.

The knot tightens as I see a flash of golden curls ride past. The rider's horse runs crookedly, her chest streaked with blood, a bullet wound near her shoulder, but the rider spurs her mercilessly. I feel Asahel within me, a silver streak in my blood, as I launch myself into

Absalom's path - following, hunting, chasing like a hound on a scent.

Absalom feels my pursuit, the infallible fear-sense of prey. His heels thud dully against his poor animal's sides; she falls, her front legs buckling. Absalom narrowly avoids being pinned beneath her weight.

The knot tightens as he scrambles to his feet and starts to run.

In shadows he flees; fear dominates his thinking, grasping for a place to hide. He heads for the oldest, deepest wood. The branches clutch at him, and he slashes at them with his knife. The branches are stronger. His knife sticks deep into a knot, and Absalom leaves it.

He is trying to duck low as he runs.

The branches are lower.

He cries out. His curls tangle in the needles, branches drag his head back, like a lover reaching for a kiss. He screams as the fear-sense alerts to him to my presence, but he cannot turn, cannot feel anything but my cold breath on the back of his neck, freezing the sweat. I pin him to the ground with a thrust of my sword.

The knot tightens with the dimming of the battle-sounds, as armies move farther and farther into the light. No matter how he screams, no one but I can hear Absalom. I circle him, crouch down before his face so that he can see the green fire in my eyes.

I rip away his royal coat, his gold-trimmed waistcoat, his soft linen shirt. My sword has pierced his heart, and the blood that bubbles to the surface is almost black with abundance. Absalom spits at me and curses, but his strength is leaving him, running with his blood into the forest floor. I press my lips to the wound and drink.

Just before he is dead, I hook my fingers in the ragged chest and tear him open. His last scream pierces my ears, but the pine trees swallow it. In the dark and the damp and rot, I eat. The knot tightens around my neck.

Bathsheba finds me first, spread over Absalom's broken body, my face and shoulders smeared with blood and flesh. For the moment, she stares. She has time to reach for her pistol, time to start running, but she does not. Instead she speaks.

"David wanted him alive," she says softly. I push myself to my knees; each breath is agony. I have no idea how far I've run. The Black Queen watches me. Her hands are folded at her stomach, graceful, almost demure, as though the stench of liver and human blood was inconsequential.

"Well," she says finally. "You have done well, Joab. We must tell your brother."

And now, Mother, the knot begins to unravel.

***

The knot unravels when I ask him, "Why do you never eat?"

Abishai smiles, his eyes closed, his head on my pillow. The window of the barracks is open, wafting in the smells of roasting meat and spilled beer—the aroma of celebration. The victory belongs to David the King.

"Because I look after you, little brother."

"I can hunt for myself. Why do you save the best men for me?"

Abishai flinches, and the knot unravels.

"The world is faltering. There are no good men, not enough for both of us. Would you eat filth? Consume cowards, and weaklings, and fools?"

"Then let me share with you."

He beckons me closer. When I sit on the bed beside him, he fists his fingers in my hair and drags me down for a kiss.

"Grow strong, little brother," he hisses. "Grow strong and brave and cunning, more than any one man can be. Bring them all into yourself. That is how you can show your gratitude."

Roughly, he thrusts me aside. The knot unravels.

After Absalom, there is Amasa. After Amasa comes Sheba. After Sheba, the gigantic Ishbi-Benob, whom David has grown too old to slay. Generals and rebels, Abners and Absaloms, their lungs sweet with cleverness and ambition, their livers spicy with strength. Like a good little soldier, I do as Abishai commands. I bring them all into myself.

The knot unravels as Abishai stands behind Bathsheba's chair, whispering something sweet and poisonous into her delicate ear. Her firm body grows round and soft with a son—the boy to whom David has promised his throne. Bathsheba closes her eyes, listening to my brother, and rubs her belly.

It unravels with a pretty boy named Benaiah, a tall, thin boy with glossy black curls. It unravels when I see Abishai whispering to him and my brother's lips slip, framing the name Asahel. I see the green absinthe flames burning in Benaiah's eyes.

"Is he one of us?" I ask Abishai. Abishai presses a cold kiss to my forehead, which is no answer at all.

The knot unravels as David lies on his deathbed, his cheek as pale as his pillow, his lips as gray as steel. Bathsheba kneels by his side, stroking his hair, but her face is not gentle. Her little boy stands at her side. Abishai hovers in the doorway. And I? I am not welcome here; I crouch beside the door, listening. Absalom is a crimson streak in my blood, frowning on David with disgust.

"He's too weak," I whisper to my brother. "I can't do it."

"But there is strength in his blood, and bravery, and cunning."

"Not anymore."

I turn my face in contempt. Abishai catches my chin in his hand.

"Please, Joab, for me."

It is now that I know, mother. The knot unravels, and I know.

They do not mean for me to overhear David's orders, but the walls are so very thin. As thin as cloth and flesh, and thin as a brother's love. I hear my name, and the name of the madman of Bahurim, whose courage Abishai has so admired. I hear Benaiah ordered to kill.

The knot is nothing but a wisp of thread.

***

"And when," I ask, "will you take your little Benaiah?"

Abishai looks up at me, his cold face all wounded innocence, but I see the blood like poison clinging to his red lips, the green fire that has always burned in his eyes when he looks at me. I throw off his embrace and stand, pressing my forehead against the barracks wall. The cool stone does nothing to cool the fire in my chest.

"Will you fat him on generals and princes and rebels and giants, as you've fatted me? And when you take him, will you kiss him and stroke his hair and remind him how much you've done for him? Or will you send someone else? Another Joab? Another Benaiah? Another good little soldier to draw all the others together, to deliver armies to you in one fragile chest?"

"This is how it must be, Joab. Please try to understand."

I do understand. I have the thread stretched between my fingers, the thread made of names: Asahel,

Abner, Absalom, Amasa. Joab, Benaiah. Abishai. But one name is missing, and I understand - one last hunt, one last meal before I die. This is the way it ends.

"Just tell me one thing, Abishai." I lift my head from the wall. "Whose idea was it? Yours, or hers?"

The tip of his tongue darts out, moistening his lips. "Whose?"

"Mother's, Abishai." And I smile at him, Asahel's joyful smile and Abner's cunning one, Absalom's beauty and Amasa's cruelty, a smile like a smear of blood.

"Our mother," I say.

He turns white, and I know that he knows.

***

This is the story I want you to hear.

***

It ends as David is dying. His breath is ragged and loping, his eyes stare glassily at the painted ceiling. They have left him alone. A moment of peace, they think, a moment to collect himself before they say goodbye.

It ends with me padding across the floor, a deeper shadow in a room full of shadows. Does he see me? Does the fear-sense prickle the hair on the back of his neck? I open his nightshirt and run my sharp-nailed fingers over his hollow chest. It ends with the blood and flesh of a king. A gift to Abishai, if I ever reach him, passing through Benaiah and countless others. The gift of strength and bravery and cunning, all beneath my fingertips, through this tiny shield of skin and flesh. It ends with this, my last hunt.

But shall I tell you a secret, mother?

This is not how the story ends.

Because I will feed them, mother. That, I cannot help. Benaiah will come for me, though I hide in the temple itself; he will come and he will spill my blood and feel the sweetness of my lungs bursting between his teeth, and he will consume me. And later—perhaps as himself, perhaps as a streak of blue in another man's blood—Benaiah will feed Abishai. And later still, at the very end of the story, Abishai will feed you.

But he will not feed you a king.

It ends with David's breath catching in his throat. He sees me, I know he sees me, and not as a shadow. My name flickers across his lips. I press my hand against his chest, feel his heart galloping, galloping, his lungs swelling feebly and sinking down to nothing. It would be so easy to rip open his chest, to taste those lungs, that pounding blood.

I kiss his lips instead, and it ends.

***

Well, my son? Is this the story you wanted to hear?

Ask him that, before he dies. A story is a knot. As it tightens, we strangle.

The Sons of Zeruiah by Megan Arkenberg

Just like hunger. Just like love.

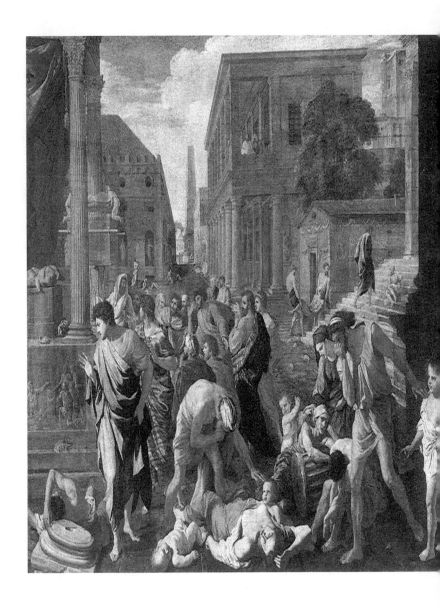

God Box
by Lyda Morehouse

When the InForcer soldiers brought the aliens' box into Kayla Okiro's sanctuary, the lights flickered. Though power fluctuations were common close to the border, no window-rattling boom of a nearby EMP bomb or concussion grenade preceded it. Kayla shivered and clutched the heavy gold cross around her neck.

The box was a hideous thing, made of a material that shone darkly metallic, like an inky hematite. Large and dense, it took six soldiers to carry it into the church. Like pallbearers, they bore the box on their shoulders. Menacing carvings covered the surface. At the ends of the box, sea serpents with rows of spike-teeth and odd arrangements of limbs rose up. Their eyes had been set with a red gem found on Ganymede's rocky outcroppings. Like carnivorous amber, the gem had trapped a creature that glowed with eerie bioluminescence.

The snakes twisted around themselves along the top as if prisoners of a sinister Chinese puzzle box.

"Why here?" she asked, barely keeping the tremor from her voice.

The soldiers did not share Kayla's sense of dread. In fact, they were jubilant. When they set the thing down on the altar they high-fived each other. Loud whoops bounced hollowly off the ceiling of the nave. From the cross, Jesus frowned. The alien container remained silent.

"Why me?" she asked, once the noise dissipated.

The commanding officer was a young man, startlingly pale for a soldier in Earth's Intergalactic Peacekeeping Force. Ganymede's radiation left pockmarks and burn scars on his cheeks and nose. "Reverend, your church is on ground that belongs to Earth. It's the next best thing to bringing it to the capitol."

The soldiers continued to congratulate themselves.

"Can you fucking believe it?"

"That fat old priestess literally fell off her throne!"

"Died on the spot when she heard the box was taken."

"She broke her own damn neck."

The commander waved his hand and shushed his soldiers' cheer. "Is there some kind of problem, Reverend?" he asked almost apologetic, "You were supposed to have received a packet of explaining."

Kayla nodded in acquiescence, though it arrived only minutes before the soldiers, containing some oblique information, mentioning an item of political significance. It spoke foremost about Kayla's duty to the System with clear implications. Do this, or we might be forced to remember all past associations from a misspent youth.

For a conclusion, the missive's robotic voice told her that the information was a mere courtesy. The

United Church, her bosses back on Earth, had signed off on the transfer.

"No. No problem, officer," she said automatically. Kayla's eyes strayed to the dark, gnarled shape on the altar. "But won't the Rovers come after it?"

"I don't know. They seemed devastated, but it's important to them." he admitted. "We'll be leaving an honor guard, for your protection, of course."

Two soldiers stepped forward at their commander's gesture. They wore the armbands marking them as members of EDC, the Elite Defense Corps.

Kayla was not comforted

She rallied a thin smile of gratitude. Having EDC under her roof complicated things. She would have to be careful. If the two soldiers sensed her inner hostility, they didn't react. Like their brethren, they acted foolishly euphoric, as if they had won the war by stealing this ugly little box. The commander smiled and the soft expression made his ruined face seem almost handsome. He put a hand on Kayla's shoulder and she stifled a flinch.

"Don't worry," he said. "We gave those Rovers a massive smack-down. We've got them on the run."

Rovers on the run? Kayla sincerely doubted his optimism.

They believed Ganymede their ancient homeland; Earth Force scientists couldn't disprove their assertion. Genetically, they had as much in common with the sea creatures swimming in Ganymede's warm underground oceans, as the colonists did with the remaining Earth species. The Rovers very well might have been cosmic cousins before, according to their legends, they left our system many centuries earlier.

Unfortunately, the frozen upper oceans of Jupiter's "cup bearer" represented the major sources of all drinkable water in Earth's system. Though water could be found on Europa and in the comet haloes, Earth saw the mere idea of an alien settlement in the center of the System as a personal affront, an invasion.

There had been war instantly.

And constantly.

The Rovers hadn't backed down either. Their gods had told them that Jupiter's watery moon was their ancient homeland. They'd wandered the stars long enough, they said. They viewed earth colonists as the interlopers.

Kayla offered her congratulations on the soldiers' victory. She made appropriate noises about food and drink; the commanding officer declined on behalf of his troops. There were a few wistful glances in her direction as the soldiers transformed their uniforms for the trip back outside, pressure seals hissing and the ozone smell filling the sanctuary.

She hugged herself, and let a hand slip into the pocket of her pants to rub at the edges of her talisman. The taller of the two EDC officers suited up as well. His dark skin was smooth and unmarked by radiation, but he had seen his share of battles. A thick white line cut through his eyebrow and split his upper eyelid. He introduced himself as Sergeant al-Farran. He explained how he would perform the preliminary patrol around the church grounds. Kayla nodded absently.

The remaining soldier, his uniform as black as the box, stood in the nave. She looked up at Jesus on the cross. His face showed only the slightest suffering, a crease in his brow. Otherwise, his expression was beatific, accepting, and serene. She took comfort from that face now, as she always did. He would not abandon her. He never had; not even in the darkest of hours.

If she had patience, the soldiers would move their war trophy eventually. Surely, if they were right, and this war had ended, they would take it on parade or send it to the capitol. Then she could go back to her real work, God's work.

Approaching the solider, Kayla smiled as sweetly as she could muster. The young man's fingers constantly and absently stroked the leather holster of his peacemaker.

"Something to drink, officer . . . ?"

"Liu," he supplied. "Corporal Liu. No, thank you, ma'am."

"Reverend," she corrected reflexively.

He nodded brusquely.

"Of course. My apologies, Reverend." He turned to regard her and the metallic buttons indicating rank and division glittered on his stiff collar. Kayla recognized the interrogator emblem to the left of his corporal insignia. She had trained her soul not to betray her alarm at the sight.

An interrogator.

Dear God!

"Please," she said quickly. "No offense taken."

For a tense moment, he said nothing. Interrogator models could detect the slightest increase in heart rate, the dilation of pupils, and dozens of adrenaline responses. She wished she were a cyborg and could control her vital signs. Finally, he shifted slightly and asked, "Would you mind if I take a look around inside, Reverend?"

"No, no, of course, go ahead. I have work to do in the office," she gestured with a hand that wasn't shaking. "I'll be in there if you need me."

***

Kayla got into her office in time to throw up into the wastebasket. She heaved until she was empty of everything except the nausea.

The last time she saw an interrogator she was fifteen.

She had been trying to forget ever since.

She pulled the talisman from her pocket. A crude cross, small enough to hide in the palm of her hands, it was fashioned from a broken piece of prison smartcrete and Martian-dust red. Onto the flattest surface she'd drawn a stick figure. Jesus' silly bearded smiley face never failed to tease out a grin. Her fingers traced the edges of the talisman, wearing down smooth corners, shiny with years of rubbing and the oil of her skin.

Kayla set the talisman down carefully on the desk. Her hands were steadier. They couldn't hurt her here. She was a grown woman, nearly twice the age she was then. The talisman had gotten her through those horrible months; it would see her through this trial.

***

Kayla had trouble sleeping.

Any time she closed her eyes, memories of the beatings and the rape returned. Isolated images and sensations broke through the years - the acrid smell of his breath, the blood red color of the walls, the creaking of the uniform's nanofabric, and the distant sounds of genengineered watchdogs barking in the courtyard. She'd left that all behind when she'd fled Mars with the other refugees. Seminary soothed and buried much of the rest.

The damned box had brought it all back.

Ganymede was tidally locked to Jupiter. During the five-day sunside cycle, light reflected constantly off the gas-giant's atmosphere. The church dimmed to simulate the day/night pattern that human beings, no matter how far removed from Earth, need. At her darkened window, Kayla could see the planet's raging red storm swirling beyond the military's defense bubble dome.

It reminded her of the glowing eyes of the box's serpents.

And Martian sand.

From her nightstand, she took the talisman and clutched it to her chest. Its familiar presence slowed her trembling heart. It calmed her to the point where she could form rational delusions of normalcy.

One simple thought pushed all others aside. If the soldiers stayed, the bandages of time and distance would fade. She would be broken again – perhaps irreparably.

She got up.

If she could convince the soldiers to move the box, there was a chance at survival.

The sanctuary seemed deserted. Kayla's fingers gripped the ornate edges of the smartcrete doorway and squinted into cavernous space. At the far end of the church, the alien box's sea serpents' eyes glowed dimly.

"Corporal Liu?"

Her voice bounced hollowly through the dark chamber. Would the interrogator still be on duty, or would they have sent a replacement? "Hello?"

The only answer was a soft scuttling – the sound of tiny, sharp nails skittering across stone.

Nothing native to Ganymede survived long on the surface. Its oceans swarmed with life, but none of it breathed air – certainly not the highly specific nitrogen/oxygen combination humans imported. Only the Rovers claimed ancestral homelands.

Kayla groped for the light switch. When she punched the night cycle override code, brightness crawled into the sanctuary. A twenty-foot, stone figure spread out on the floor in the open space before the altar, like a supplicant.

She was confused until she saw the empty cross. The statue Jesus Christ had come off the crucifix and bowed down before the aliens' box.

She didn't even realize she'd been screaming until the InForcer soldiers rushed in with guns drawn. Corporal Liu gently pulled her up into onto her feet. She clutched at him, desperately, suddenly grateful for his imposing strength.

Seeing the statue, Al-Farran swore softly in Arabic. "Who would do this?" he asked no one in particular. Tapping the side of his temple, he issued commands, "Initiate perimeter lock down. APB for . . ." he struggled momentarily to describe the desecration "possible vandals."

"That crucifix was solid marble," Lui said, his arm casually and protectively circled her, as if he was accustomed to hysterical women sobbing into his nano-armored uniform.

Her stomach soured at the thought.

She pulled away sharply, the scent of his uniform cloying at the back of her throat. Kayla struggled not to gag. She wiped her eyes. "Yes, it is . . . was . . . an imported antique from Earth."

"That'll be difficult to replace. I'm sorry for your loss," he said sympathetically, automatically. "Do you have any idea who might have had the skill to do this?"

"Skill?"

He approached the body of Jesus, and pointed as he spoke, "Look how the shoulders are rounded, not flat or hacked like you'd expect when separating stone in a hurry. Most bizarre to me," he added, Kayla following along like a lost lamb as he climbed the steps of the dais and stood directly under the empty cross, "is that there's no dust. Telemetry detects zero marble particles in the air. Not a single flake or stone chip has been left anywhere. These vandals of yours not only brought a ladder, but a fucking shop vac too."

Al-Farran gave his subordinate a sharp glance.

"Pardon my French, ma'am. Sir," Liu said with a deferent nod.

Kayla shook her head to show she wasn't offended. She stood beside the aliens' box; looked up at the smooth surface of the cross. Kayla couldn't shake the suspicion that God Himself had come down off the cross to supplicate before the hideous thing.

Beside her, a rattling thing hissed from the container. Kayla jumped back.

"Is there something alive in there?" she asked.

"No, absolutely not," Al-Farran said. He was crouching in Jesus' armpit. "We had it scanned and x-rayed in the field. We weren't going to let the Rovers go all Trojan horse on us."

The sea serpents' glowing eyes trapped Kayla's gaze. The metallic head faced a different direction yesterday. Blinking, she moved her eyes away from the hypnotizing light.

"You don't think the box had anything to do with this?" Liu asked her.

"No," she said quickly, trying to control her growing unease. "How could it?"

***

A crew of twenty in heavy mech-suits, two portable cranes, and a high-powered dust management filter removed Jesus from the church. The statue was too heavy to be lifted as a single piece, so they took sledgehammers to Christ's body. Kayla couldn't watch.

From an exalted position upon His altar, the box presided over Jesus' eviction. Kayla sensed smug satisfaction in the toothy grins of its sea serpent decorations.

Of course, the InForcers used the incident as an excuse to bring in more soldiers. A plague of EDC officers, with their menacing double-sword lapel pins, infested the church grounds.

An EDC commander - a colonel with sharp, beady black eyes - stood over her desk, his hands clasped behind his back. She knew better than to trust his relaxed pose. The silence between them was fraught with implications.

"You were a member of the Martian resistance," he said again. His voice was soft and friendly.

Kayla was having trouble remembering to breathe. She reached for the comfort of the talisman in her

King David and the Spiders from Mars

pocket. She could deny the truth, but she might as well deny Christ.

"I was fifteen. I served my time. I spoke the oath."

"Yes, you did," he said slowly. "I understand that you were difficult to re-educate."

Re-educate? Is that what they called it? It had taken them two full weeks to break her. A record, she discovered later. She'd kept her soul intact by singing hymns and rebel songs - to herself - in her cell - at night, until the guards discovered that her music was giving the other prisoners hope. Without anger or joy, they broke her jaw and numbed her vocal cords. She hadn't been able to scream when the interrogators raped her.

She had taken the pledge as soon as she could talk.

But she had survived without a voice, because the talisman-Jesus continued to smile. He loved her. No matter how dirty and disgusting she felt, Jesus would not abandon her.

Kayla knew her body had betrayed her the moment the cyborg stepped into the room. Even so, she looked away, past the two guards standing just outside the open doorway into the sanctuary at the black box on the altar. "What does this have to do with the vandalism?"

"Are you still a rebel?" he asked. "Do you have friends who would work mischief with our war trophy?"

"I would never defile the church!" Kayla found herself standing, momentarily allowing insult to overcome terror. Her hand clutched her talisman even as its edges cut into her palms. Her voice became calm and detached. "Regardless of any residual feelings I might have toward you InForcers."

"You really should learn to use the proper term for the Peacekeeping Force. We might get the wrong impression."

"Fuck you," she said. The guards straightened their postures and became very attentive.

He raised a single eyebrow.

"Indeed."

Kayla waited for more guards to storm in and take her away in handcuffs, but, strangely, the EDC colonel dismissed the guards with a nod. He graced Kayla a quick a smile that approached something resembling actual warmth. "Now that we've dispensed with the games, perhaps I can trust you with information about the Rover's coffer."

She nodded mutely, too stunned to do more than relax back into her seat.

"I understand Sergeant al-Farrar told you that we examined the coffer in the field."

Fear crept up her spine.

"Yes. He assured me that it was empty."

The colonel grimaced.

"It is. Technically. It's not so much what is in the coffer, as what it represents."

Kayla could feel the blood draining from her face. "What's that?"

"From what we can decipher, the Rovers believe a piece of their god is inside the box."

The image of Jesus lying down before the altar flashed into her mind. She shook her head. He nodded, as though agreeing with her silent thoughts. "This is all nonsense. Gods don't exist." The colonel paused for a moment, "Except ours, of course."

He was not a believer, Kayla could tell by how quickly he added the addendum. The colonel watched her face. He seemed to be looking for something. Finally, he said, "Our God is real. He is stronger than their god."

He didn't dare say it, but his eyes held the question mark. Her palms stung from where the talisman edges cut her skin. She knew the answer without hesitation.

"God has never abandoned me."

"Then all is well."

For much of the rest of the afternoon, it was.

Kayla watched the box while the soldiers waited and the mech crew finished sweeping away the last traces of Jesus. She couldn't quite get rid of the feeling that something sentient inside the box stared back at her.

When the radiation alarm sounded, the soldiers activated their uniforms quickly, but Kayla and the mech crew were caught unprepared. Kayla rushed to her desk and took the skin patches. She had had enough for the congregation, which meant that she could barely accommodate the mech crew. When she was certain that everyone was patched, she spoke with an authority that had not been in her voice since the box came to desecrate the sanctuary.

"Everyone without armor, please follow me to the basement shelter."

The shelter was tiny. They sat on the floor, hugging knees and elbows to keep from jostling one another, and waited for the klaxon to stop. Kayla's scalp itched. Jammed together with so many anxious people, her body rocked back and forth with the memory of the Martian camps. Her sanity frayed with voices, screams and rebel songs, once comforting but now sinister. She closed her mouth and didn't speak, afraid of what would come if she allowed words to emerge.

***

"It wasn't an attack," the colonel assured her afterwards when they all filed out. "HQ reported a random glitch in the bubble. These happen from time to time."

She nodded absently. The bubble had malfunctioned so much in the early days that she'd worn a protection suit under her vestments every day. She felt lightheaded and her clothes were soaked with nervous sweat. Kayla gratefully went to the mandatory, if useless, shower without speaking to the colonel further.

She stripped as the water heated. Kayla caught sight of her reflection in the mirror on the back of the door, and gasped. Blisters – stage two ulcerations –

covered her back in an s-shape, curving along her spine, like a snake.

Or a sea serpent.

It wasn't possible. Her exposure had lasted no more than a few minutes. She continued to inspect herself in disbelief; she noticed an oval spot on her right shoulder blade. It bled, bright crimson blood like the eye of the box's guardian. When the soldiers broke down the door, she did not know that she was screaming.

***

By middle night cycle, the sanctuary had become a field hospital. Bodies filled the pews. Every member of the mech crew exhibited symptoms. The two crane operators were already dead. Patients vomited blood into buckets, and advanced necrosis permeated the air. The aliens' box remained shrouded in semi-darkness. Kayla had turned on the spotlight used during Christmas Eve mass to illuminate the cross, but Jesus' absence gnawed at her and she had to turn it off. The red-hot eyes of the box's guardians glared from the cavernous nave; followed her as she wandered among the sick and dying.

The medics that had come with the new battalion of InForcers had assured Kayla that she would live. She'd gotten her medicine in time. Under the blisters, the skin would harden to white scar tissue. However, the 'eye' continued to bleed. They had no answer for why it soaked through a bandage every hour. They gave her blood thickener pills and told her not to worry. She'd come out so much better than the rest. She'd be permanently marked, forever branded with the strange image on her back, but she would survive.

She no longer bothered hiding her talisman. She clutched it in her fist, held it close to her heart. Often, she would stop and kiss the smiley face Jesus - the only representation of Him left to her in this horrible place.

A blinded worker reached out for her as she passed the woman's pew. Kayla flinched. She knew what the woman would say; all the mech crew asked the same question, "Is this my fault? Because I smashed Jesus?"

Kayla had comforted them at first, reminded them of God's boundless love, until she noticed a curious pattern - the stronger the confession, the worse the injury. The man who said, "I took a sledgehammer to His face! Ai, Madre!" had no part of his skin that wasn't dead-black. Open wounds dripped sticky puss-filled globs that soaked the white sheet and spattered the marble floor yellow-red. He wouldn't last the night. His death would be slow.

Had God done this?

This was not the kind and loving God she knew, the one who had carefully tended her battered and wounded soul.

She was beginning to wonder if she knew God at all.

She felt eyes on her, and she looked up to see the rat-faced colonel. He leaned against a wall, his arms crossed in front of his chest. His black gaze bore into her; she could almost hear his voice asking: "Our God is stronger than theirs, isn't He?"

The black box glittered in the darkness.

Nausea hit Kayla hard, and she turned and fled.

She ran to the garden in the back of the church grounds. The day-cycle slowly lightened the courtyard. The green space served as a cemetery; stones marked with the names the faithful formed a waterfall in the middle of the space. Kayla inhaled the smells of artifacts painstakingly transferred from Earth - loamy dirt, fecund mulch, vegetables and edible flowers. Bees buzzed from one trembling blossom to the next.

Kayla knelt in the dirt. Bowing her head to pray for guidance, she took the talisman out to bring it to her lips. She sought the comfort of the crude depiction of Jesus, needing that silly, kind smile now more than ever.

It was gone.

She flipped the cross over, thinking she must have been holding it wrong. The other side was blank, as well.

It wasn't possible. Though she'd rubbed it more today than she had in a long time; no way could she have erased Jesus. The image was bonded to the stone on a molecular level. After smuggling the talisman out of prison, she'd taken the precaution to have the image permanently sealed to the smartcrete. She'd paid dearly for nano-technician to reactivate the bots long enough to incorporate her sketch into the rock.

She blinked. Rubbed the tears from her face and searched the tiny x-shaped stone, turning it over in her hands.

Why would He leave her now?

Behind her, someone cleared his throat. The rat colonel had come to infest her last quiet refuge.

"I'm sorry to disturb your prayer, Reverend," he said. "But perhaps I bear good news. We're moving the coffer."

"What?" Kayla's fingers continued to rub the spot on the make-shift crucifix where the smiley-face should have been.

"Yes. We're going now."

He headed for the door. Kayla stood to follow him, her mind struggling to understand what was happening. She shambled after him, feeling empty. "But, I don't understand...."

"Of course we'll remove anyone who lives through the night. Our medical team will make sure they get to the best hospitals. We'll help you bury the dead."

"But...."

They had returned to the sanctuary. The moans and cries of the suffering filled the church like a baleful choir. On the dais, six grim-faced soldiers heaved the box onto their shoulders.

The colonel turned to Kayla. "You were wrong. Your god is no match for theirs. Al-Farran has convinced me to take the box to a mosque. Perhaps Allah will fare better."

Words failed Kayla. The muscles in her legs trembled, and she fell, kneeling, to the hard marble floor.

There, she saw it.

The tiny stick figure was on the floor, face down. Hair obscured the smiley face. The black lines dark on the marble, as if it had always been there, deep in the rock's veins - its simple arms outstretched in supplication to the alien box.

Chabad of Innsmouth
by Marsha Morman

My name is Menachem Schneuri, and I had never heard of Innsmouth until the day I was posted there.

"Massachusetts fishing town." Rabbi Greenberg's file contained only a few sparsely-worded pages. "About an hour from Providence. Same from Boston. You should be able to make it back to the Rebbe's kever in Brooklyn in five hours if the traffic's quiet on I-95." He was going over the material, and I watched his eyes dart back and forth across the print-out.

"The community there is Russian immigrants and their children. When they first came over, most of the bunch went to Providence, and some of them are regulars at the Hope Street center run by Rabbi Grossbaum. But a few stragglers wound up in this little village. Now that housing prices are rising in East Providence, they've gotten some regulars from Chabad of Providence to migrate. They should all speak English now, more or less, and maybe a little Yiddish. But the important point is they want their own center, and they put the money up for it."

He closed the manila folder and passed it to me.

"And without us even having to ask. A gift from Hashem himself."

It did very much seem that way. I wasn't expecting a good posting. I lacked the family connections to join a big center with an established community or even a new one in a decent location. To say I squeaked by on my Rabbinic exams is putting it lightly. If I was unmarried, I might even expect to be posted in some third-world country, making the best I could with a couple siddurs and crates of canned tuna fish. My wife had a cousin posted in Kathmandu, where the Chabad-Lubavitch Outreach Center catered to Israeli backpackers, and he stretched out a single chicken to feed fifty people with soup using old bullions. But a posting on the Eastern seaboard! Within hours of kosher food and other Hasids! And we could come home for the holidays and visit the Rebbe's grave!

"It sounds wonderful," I said.

"You should call Rabbi Grossbaum, though I don't know how much he can tell you. He says he's never been there. He made some excuse for a scouting trip to meet the community. Everything's been done over emails and wire transfers. But I've heard from him that it's supposed to be a little run down. Not a place where tourists go to see the colors."

He could sense my enthusiasm.

"You might run into some fundraising difficulties, with such a small community, but we're prepared for that. The donor was very insistent that you'll be given whatever you need from the locals. We'll see how that promise holds up with the economy, or if the price of gold drops. The whole donation was in gold jewelry. Very strange story. Talk to Mendel Yosef in accounting. He knows what's up."

While I'd always thought receiving my outreach assignment, a life posting for a married man looking to set up his family among assimilated Jews secretly yearning for a touch of Yiddishkeit in their lives, would be more dramatic than an almost-empty folder from Rabbi Greenberg's office, I wasn't one to complain.

"I'm so happy. And Toba will be happy too."

He shook my hand with his meaty fist. "Much hatzlochah to you, Menachem. You may think it's all well and good, but we're at the mercy of Hashem's plans for us. You should remember that."

***

Mendel Yosef was out to lunch, so I tried Toba, only to get her voicemail. She was cooking with her mother no doubt, so I decided the good news could wait and asked to use an office computer at 770 while I waited for the accounting whiz to return. The internet modesty filter sometimes blocked Wikipedia, and I wasn't about to tamper with the settings, but the page for Innsmouth came up easily enough. The solitary picture was marked "Old Town" and gave a view of the city from what must have been out in a ship on the water. The inky shoreline was visible at the bottom. I recognized the architecture as the New England style of homes I had passed on my way up to retreats – tall church spires, two-level buildings along one-way streets, and cobblestone. Even though the picture was dated to the 1920's, its quality still allowed me to notice the lack of color shades between the buildings and even peeling paint on some walls. The picture didn't provide color in the first place, but it seemed as though the whole town might have really been . . . well, grey. The houses were too cluttered, the trees too bare as if the leaves had been torn off instead of naturally fallen, and attic windows were boarded up. The only building with more than three stories stood at the very stop of the hill. It must have been some kind of hotel. The two darkened circular windows on the top floor gave it the appearance that it was staring at me.

With undefined anxiety, I moved quickly back to the text. Founded in 1643, the town was known for shipbuilding and manufacturing until a plague killed most of the population in 1846. In 1927 – possibly before the photograph was taken – a major raid on an illegal bootlegging industry yielded dozens of arrests. As for information about the town since then, I found almost nothing. Population: Unknown. Unknown? Didn't the government at least count people?

A more extensive internet search brought up some color pictures of construction in "New Town" with more familiar buildings in comforting red bricks. There were no banner ads for local businesses or even rudimentary travel brochures for people sick of the highway drive. The sole indication of any life beyond the manicured trees of New Town was an ad for the Marsh Fish Market, with its two convenient locations.

My fingers took me back to the first page and the picture of Innsmouth at its height. The roads curved their way down to the sea and the hotel stood alone against the sky.

"Menachem?"

Mendel Yosef's voice brought me out of a shock. A cold sweat was forming for no identifiable reason, but I followed him into his office and put it out of my mind. This was money we were talking about, money Toba and I would need to live and do our kiruv work.

Mendel Yosef was all business.

"This wasn't a location we were considering. Not many families, most of them go to the Chabad House in Providence if they are interested. But with the donation we got . . ." He shook his head. "So look at this." He held up a full-color print of a gold, gem encrusted necklace and what I thought was – well, it wasn't a choker. More like a headband, with a massive ruby in the center. My little knowledge of jewelry told me the design was foreign, and the picture wasn't good enough to make out the engravings, which looked like a wave design.

"The guy's name is Yuri, but don't worry, you won't have to meet him. I only spoke to him over the phone after he sent the pieces in the mail, and no insurance or delivery confirmation! He was one of the Russians – there's maybe five or six of them left – who moved straight to Innsmouth after the Soviets let them out. I'm not even sure he's really Jewish. He married a local girl, a non-Jew obviously, and when she died he sent us the jewelry and said maybe we could lend our services to some of the newer people. I didn't talk to him long, because a day later his phone was disconnected. When I finally got in touch with a friend, they said he moved to Israel, just like that. But I really did try to find him, because of the pieces. Looks like gold, doesn't it?"

"It's brass?"

"We don't know what it is. From afar, yes, it's gold, but it's got this shiny gloss over it that makes it sparkle almost like my son's watch, the one where the numbers glow for a few minutes after you turn the lights out at night. I took it to 47th Street to have the gems inspected, and they didn't know what to make of them. This Satmar claims he spent so long staring at this one diamond he hurt his eye. They can't tell us what it's worth because they don't know the carats or anything. I thought about it a few days and I notice it's got these inscriptions, and I start thinking about them. It's all fish and waves and these weird islands. So you know where I took it? The Met. Let an art expert give it a try. I went with the suitcase with the handcuff to my wrist and everything.

"Two weeks go by and I get a call from the curator. She says it's Polynesian. Maybe."

"Where?"

"South Asia. Or they've found a bunch of pieces like this there, with the glimmering gold – luminescence is the word she used. And by 'they' I mean the world. There's only twelve known pieces, mostly headbands or bracelets, in different museums across Europe - except for one in Newburyport, the town one over from Innsmouth. This is when I started calling around, trying to find people who knew Yuri, or knew his wife, and no one in Innsmouth can tell me anything. I can't think of what else to do with it, so 770 put it on the open market, and it went for 3.5 million dollars to the National Museum of Denmark - for their East Asian collection. Can you believe it?"

There was no reason to disbelieve it, but I could still be shocked. Three-point-five million for two pieces of gold and some rocks? That was going to pay for my house in Innsmouth and a lot of free Shabbos dinners for the community.

"I don't think fundraising's going to be an issue if you stretch that money. There's a seminar on money management for shliachs and shluchim that you and your wife should take. In a few years, down the road, sure, but everyone has those problems. It's all being handled by Pavel. He's also one of the originals, married to a shiksa, but what can you do? He's setting up everything. He knows you'll need a lot of rooms and large indoor spaces, and he's very, very eager for you come – to see the place, sign some paperwork, that sort of thing. When can you be available?"

My only possible answer could be, "When do you need me?"

***

Toba was as overjoyed – and relieved – as I was.

"And we'll never be far from the Grossbaums in Providence, and they have seven children already," I assured her. "There's nothing in Innsmouth but a clinic, but there's a good hospital in Providence if it should come to that, G-d forbid."

She tried not to make an issue of it, but her belly was starting to grow and not from her mother's chulent. We had only told her mother because it was so early, but we were married for a year now, so people might be assuming. Now, it seemed we might be settled in our new home when the baby came. And we weren't driving cross-country or flying or learning a new language, although I would probably have to pick up more Russian than I knew already, depending on how fluent in English the community was. That I was sure I could handle, with all the gifts Hashem had already given me.

"So what's this town? I've never heard of it," she said over dinner, leftovers from Shabbos lunch.

"I don't really know anything about it. A little fishing town. Mostly I know the housing is cheap and the jewelry is expensive."

I told her the story of the donor, of course, and showed her the photograph. Her reaction was not what I expected. "That's disgusting."

"You think rubies and diamonds are disgusting? I'm a lucky man."

"I'm not kidding. Get it out of my face." But she was smiling a little. "Did you go on Wikipedia?"

"At the office computer."

"That's no good. Go on our computer and turn the filter off. Then go on talkback and see what people tried to post about it before the moderators erased it. It's not loshen horah if it's not about people."

I wanted to correct her notions about evil gossip, but I did as I was told. As soon as the dishes were done, I followed links until pages came up with rejected information for the Wikipedia page, which I now noticed was locked. Since new revisions weren't allowed, all of the discussions were old. The topics were even older. People consistently tried to change the page's history to say "hundreds" of people were arrested during Prohibition instead of "dozens" and, in one case, "thousands." An incomplete paragraph about pirate gold caught my eye, but I couldn't go any further in that direction.

Conspiracy theorists were all over the place, saying the town was diseased or deformed by toxic waste, and the government covered it up by faking charges of liquor smuggling to benefit its industrial plants. Three or four times I saw something about the Esoteric Order of Dagon, some Catholic worship as far as I could tell. There was no way to keep track of all of those Christian saints. Another search revealed nothing about the order itself, just a useless link to the Assyro-Babylonian fertility god mentioned in the Books of Yehoshua and Shoftim.

The idea that people didn't like the government on the internet wasn't new to me, so I shut down the computer and turned in for the night. Toba was already asleep in her own bed, so my tossing and turning wouldn't bother her.

I got very little sleep that night and I dreamt of Mendel Yosef with a fish head.

***

I thought the paperwork would be slower, but in two weeks I was driving up to Innsmouth to sign deeds and apply for business permits. Toba was packing when I left. My stepfather gave me a gift of cassette recordings from the Rebbe's final lectures to listen to on my way up. It was sunny and most of the drive was highway driving, so I could relax to Rebbe's reassuring Yiddish call to duty for every Lubavitcher. With the help of Hashem (and the Rebbe), we would succeed in bringing Judaism to Jews. Anything was possible.

The directions were emailed from Pavel, who said Google maps did not have an accurate layout of the back roads in this county. I saw signs for Providence, Mystic, and even faraway Boston, but nothing for Innsmouth. It was the exit after Kingsport and the sign only listed the number.

NO OUTLET was written beneath it in spray paint.

Off the highway, I saw a number of turns and ramps, all of which seemed to lead me back the way I came. I looped twice before finding the only road not encouraging a U-turn. I did need gas, but the only station was closed. Beyond a boarded-up restaurant, the forest became increasingly wooded. They didn't have trees like this in Brooklyn, with thick limbs reaching out.

I switched off the cassette player so I could concentrate on the directions, but after ten minutes of woodland driving I nervously put the radio on and settled for a generic music station that slowly drifted into static. There was no way to be entirely sure I hadn't driven away from the human world. Finally, the first shacks appeared, maybe hunting lodges, mostly wood or just lonely brick fireplaces surrounded by rubble. I made the first right turn when it became available, after the sky emerged from the disappearing canopy and the town announced its presence with building after building. Pavel warned me in the email that Old Town was not much to look at. Between buildings, I caught sight of the ocean, but a dusty cloud obscured my view.

Beyond the first newly-painted houses, I turned onto a street that had a name – New Road – and a visible sign and I descended into the inappropriately named "Heights" of Innsmouth, where signs of life shot up in abundance. The streets weren't precisely crowded, but parking lots had cars. People with groceries shuffled along the newly-paved streets. The man I was meeting was fairly descriptive about his house, packed together in a condo-like structure, less like a New England cottage and more like convenient apartments for transients and limited budgets. When I was fairly sure I had at the very least the right block, I parked.

The smell that I thought might be something in the car, assaulted me before I was fully standing. It was like Chinatown on a hot afternoon, and it was everywhere, as if my car was surrounded by crawling crabs and flopping trout and disease.

"Rabbi Schneuri?" A sturdy-looking man walked across his tiny front yard to greet me. Bent over in revulsion was not the best position from which to greet a welcoming hand, but he didn't seem surprised. "Yes, I know. You get used to it. It's not even that bad here, not like Old Town." He smiled and offered me a handkerchief to cover my mouth until we got inside.

"Menachem, please," I said as we shook hands and went directly into his apartment, which seemed to be both the ground and possibly the floor above it. The air was better inside because it smelled at least of old furniture, which was a vast improvement. After a minute or so, I was ready to accept black tea in a paper cup.

My host asked me about the drive. He was straining to be pleasant. It wasn't a bad thing. He seemed, like many hardened immigrants, to be a man unaccustomed to hosting duties but trying desperately to make up for it. He had a wedding ring on but said nothing about her at all, and of course I didn't bring up the subject. He was stout, a little round maybe, and he settled into his hand-me-down chair that had the look and smell of many years in thrift store back rooms, like it was designed for his exact body type. When people didn't have much, at least what they had could have former beauty. This I could respect. The cushion next to me had traces of intricate embroidery even my mother wasn't capable of. I talked a little about myself – my years of study, why I wanted to be a shliach, and that I had a brief stint after high school slaughtering chickens in Pennsylvania for the largest kosher slaughterhouse before deciding that life would be better if I wasn't killing chickens all day. But it paid well, and I went home on weekends, so I wasn't broke in Rabbinical school or when I met Toba.

"People don't eat chicken so much here. They eat fish," Pavel said. His accent was impressively suppressed. "But it isn't kosher, I know."

"It can't be all shellfish."

"The fish from Innsmouth waters isn't kosher, no matter what it is. But this is a long story." And it didn't sound like he wanted to tell it. "Rabbi Grossbaum I don't know, but some of the younger people do, and he says he can get food for you."

"Yes. You don't have to worry about that at all. We'll cook for everyone."

"We should go now to the city hall," he said rather abruptly. Maybe he was watching the clock. "People who were born here don't like outsiders, but they like money. It should be OK."

He suggested we swing by my prospective house and Chabad center but said it wouldn't take long because it was being renovated and wasn't much to look at.

I drove and Pavel directed. He did not point out any of the possible sites of interest. He was right about the house, too, but it was nice to see the number of the rooms and get a sense of the size. Walls were torn down so the bottom floor was just a few large rooms, one that could be a synagogue and another for hosting meals, with two more floors of small rooms for guests and future children as well as a master bedroom for Toba and myself. It wasn't unknown for our families to outgrow our houses quickly, even with two children to a room, but six bedrooms was enough to start. With all the windows open for ventilation, I noticed that the fishy smell was either not as bad or I was getting used to it.

From these heights we drove back up another hill to the center of Old Town, or at least what must have been city center. The view of the ocean was clear and the buildings a unique grey achieved only by a combination of peeling paint and constant clouds of dust. I could see why. Many of the streets were unevenly paved or not paved at all, from the looks of it. No one ventured to walk on the streets.

Desperate to make conversation I said, "What do they do here aside from fishing?" I knew he worked for a fracking company, but that was well outside of town.

"Refine gold," Pavel said definitively. "The big house at the top."

It was the building from the internet and I felt like I was driving into a picture. Without a cloud in the sky, the sun still dimmed, and I checked my watch to be sure we still had daylight. Some of the more prominent stores had fresh signs, but the colors were fading.

"Is everyone in church?" I asked as I looked for a place to park. The building next to city hall was definitely a church, even if it wasn't as stark white as the ones I passed on the way up to New England and had no steeple. The sign was missing some letters and read, "ESOTERIC ORDER OF D GON MORNING MASS 6AM."

"Yuri said you weren't allowed in churches, you Hasidic Jews," Pavel said, and I noticed a nervous tremor in his voice, over what I couldn't decide. Maybe his generous but departed friend.

"We have a custom not to go in churches, yes. I just don't see a lot of people around."

"They wouldn't want to see you. Park anywhere." He was impatient to get this particular task over with and I finally picked a spot in front of the building with the round top that was City Hall. The stench was nearly unbearable, but I wasn't going to get my handkerchief out. I did see two kids unwrapping candy outside the grocery store, and they stared as oddly at my black coat and hat. Their modern clothing but bare feet puzzled me. If Pavel hadn't rushed me in, I would have sworn they were as grey as the wall behind them.

Even though his English was technically less fluent, Pavel spoke to the man at the desk, and I looked around the lobby, which was strangely designed for an office building. A plaque explained that it had once been a hotel called the Gilman House.

Pavel called me over, and I had my first up-close look at the man across from me. His face was very unpleasant - more oval than round, with his small ears flattened against his bald head. He had a nasty green discoloration on his skin, mostly around the neck and behind the ears, but he didn't scratch or pick at it, so it must have been an old problem. He stared at me unblinkingly for as long as it took to register disgust and pointed a long finger at the signature line. He was obviously eager for me to be gone, and I was eager to go, so we finished the registration paperwork in what must have been record time. It was unwholesome to find someone so visually repellant. I was taught to look to the neshama – soul – of every person instead of their outsides. I was very ashamed as we hurried back to the car, Pavel's smelly set of keys in hand.

"He wasn't an anti-Semite," Pavel assured me. "I bet he doesn't know what a Jew is. Outsiders – you know. That's all it is."

"I believe you," I answered, which was true, but that didn't prevent me from gunning out of there and kicking up quite a bit of grey dust when I did.

My overnight stay on Pavel's couch was the last I saw of Innsmouth for three months. He did have a wife, but she did not come downstairs, even for dinner. Pavel ate an indefinable dish, and I had my pre-packed kosher food. I needed caffeine in the morning, but made a hasty exit anyway and settled for a bottle of cold Starbucks coffee at a rest stop in Connecticut. I tried not to admit to myself that I was relieved to be away from my new home, and I certainly didn't say it.

It wouldn't matter anyway – I would be bringing Toba and we would have relatives come in to help out, and we would fill our home with the smell of baking challah and cooking chulent and order our gefilte fish from Boston. I played down Old Town for my wife and her family and stuck to things that were true but neutral, like how the house was very large and pleasant and the financials would be taken care of for several years. We could really focus on building a home and little community there before other things could arise.

Before we knew it, Passover was over and it was moving day. I enlisted two of my brothers to join us. They stayed for two weeks, working hard to move furniture, set up shelving, and do anything to eliminate the fishy smell from the house. With a mixture of scented candles and Toba's cooking, we were able to hold back the tide until we were all adjusted.

Toba was the most affected, but it was difficult to tell with her condition. She was sick like she had been in the first trimester, which we thought had passed.

Even when the smells of fresh-baked bread and roast chicken dominated, she would turn green for no reason. She kept up in all this because what else could she do? This wouldn't be the last child she had at Innsmouth. We played some nervous phone tag with her obstetrician, but nothing alarmed him.

My main concern, beyond the initial problems of kashering the home, was to begin to build the community. My brothers remained there to help us make a minyan of ten Jewish men at least for Shabbos, and I was happy to find that they weren't needed on my first Friday night. Six young immigrants from the Providence community appeared, fans of Grossbaum's style at Chabad of Hope Street and obviously happy to have me there. Beyond the hanging sheet were three women, marital status unknown, but Toba would handle that part.

With them alone we would have only been nine, but precisely at the posted time on the doorway, five hardened men entered, led by Pavel. These elder Russians, the first wave of immigration to our little town, had pitted faces and widening waists. They said nothing but took their places. They held prayer books during the services but did not read from them. I was too ecstatic about their presence to care.

It continued like this beyond the first two weeks. Every week, on Fridays and Saturdays, we made that minyan. If I announced a service in emails and on the posterboard outside my door, they appeared on time, took their newly-established places in the second row, and waited out the service while the rest of us prayed with our minyan. When the Russians were separated by seating at meals, I could get a few words, usually about their jobs (they worked in the refinery) or their health, but when they were together a barrier went up between them and us. Toba invited their wives to a women's study group, but none appeared.

It was on my way out of town – to Providence, to get Toba a check-up with her new doctor – that I finally cornered Pavel on the sidewalk. Was it that they were unfamiliar with religion? Because that was common with Russians raised under Communism. I knew that. The younger guys learned the basics in Providence or flubbed their way through prayers, but it's easy to learn when you're young. Was I doing something wrong?

Pavel did not seem to want to be harsh, but his voice was very stern, "Rabbi, we invited you here because we want you here. We want there to be a synagogue and we want there to be a minyan and a Torah reading. But we did it for other people, not us. The young people . . . we're not those people, Rabbi. We're Innsmouth folk now."

He walked off, not leaving me time to contradict him.

We spent most of our time in Innsmouth, but Toba and even I found more and more reasons to go to Providence or even Newyburyport. While preparing for the Shavous holiday, we gave ourselves one Shabbos off and stayed the whole weekend at Chabad of Hope Street. Toba said she felt better there but tried not to dwell too much on that idea. I got to know Rabbi Grossbaum and his son-in-law, the one running Chabad of College Hill. Grossbaum was a model Chabad Rabbi, a big, warm guy who was always happy to be wherever he was. He wore a button that said DIVINE PROVIDENCE and could make anything sound like holy work. He wasn't too surprised about the attitude of the older Innsmouth Russians. The people who grew up under Stalin were different from the Russians who grew up under Gorbachev and glasnost. They had harder shells, but in time, I would reach them. And they were already coming to services! Such a mitzvah.

Though we had conversations over the phone and while I was running errands, it was over that Shabbos that I finally got to talk to Rabbi Grossbaum. We stayed up late singing with the many guests, fifty or sixty at peak, and we talked Torah while the Rabbi's maid cleaned up in the kitchen and our wives went to sleep. Toba was feeling stronger and I was happy about that, and it was a long time before the conversation returned to Innsmouth. He stopped me almost immediately.

"This is not Shabbos conversation," he said. "Ask me again tomorrow night, why don't you? Even if I'm tired."

I had to let it go, and even succeeded in forgetting about it through most of Saturday, but when Shabbos was over and people were racing to their computers and their activities, I didn't forget. It was rather late, because the sun was setting later, but the Rabbi only needed a gentle nudging. He took me down into his computer room.

"There's some talk," he said. "Nothing that really concerns you. Nothing you should be worried about. But there's something you should know about Innsmouth."

I sat not-so-patiently and nodded.

"I didn't know this either. Just last week, actually, I found out from a man who used to ride a bus that stopped there. I buy vegetables from him and I said I had a cousin at Innsmouth and he was all serious like, until he found out you were a rabbi and you were new. It's different now, but it used to be a very strange town."

I decided not to tell him what I thought of it now.

"The local goyim, they don't like Innsmouth folk. They say they have a funny look and they smell bad. But it used to be much worse. I think it was, maybe a hundred years ago, during Prohibition . . . "

"There was a government raid on liquor," I interrupted.

"That's what you heard too? Because I started reading online after I spoke to this guy, and that's what it said. Bottlenecking."

"Bootlegging."

"Yes, that. But it wasn't that. It had nothing to do with that. There was a cult in Innsmouth – not a Christian one or one of these Wiccan things the college kids do. The Esoteric Order of Dagon. It sounds like one of those community groups where the men get together and wear red fezzes, right? But it wasn't. It was bad. I don't know what they really did, but the grocer said it was Satanic. And it went on for a while, too. Sixty or seventy years. That's how they got all their gold, deals with Satan and that nonsense. But during Prohibition, the government got wind of it. Now I know the government tolerates all kinds of crazy things in this country, including what we do, but this was just beyond. They rounded up the whole town and sent them to prison. The town was emptied, and whatever you see now, he said you can tell the difference between their descendents who escaped and people who moved in since. Can you?"

My throat went dry and I didn't answer him. I didn't want to speak ill of anybody. And I was also very afraid.

"That's why their real estate is so cheap. There had to be a reason, right? Because the town's never recovered. Hopefully, the new town you live in will split off from the old town entirely, or that's what my informant hoped. This is a guy, he's very nice, very open-minded. Not Jewish but is always going on about how he checked all the vegetables for bugs before he sold them to me just because he liked me. He's interested. He's even a little worldly. But he said to me, 'Don't mix with the Innsmouth folk. Don't have anything to do with them. And don't let your cousin do it, either.' And I was just shocked at the way he said it."

He let silence sit in the air for what must have been a full minute before the rabbi cleared his throat. "The older immigrants, they intermarried?"

"I haven't met their wives. Neither has Toba."

He nodded and put a hand on my shoulder. "You're going to do great work there. Hashem has a plan, sending you there. They need you more than you think."

***

I wish Rabbi Grossbaum's speech had been a turning point for me and Toba. Perhaps it was, but not in the right way. We could only keep our spirits so high as Toba's pregnancy progressed. It was normal for her not to be a picture of health while carrying a child, but from our trips to nearby towns, Providence, and one trip back to Brooklyn, it was obvious that she was better outside of Innsmouth. I tried all sorts of air purifiers and had a back-up carbon monoxide alarm complementing the current one, but nothing made much of a difference. She would get weak again and be sick in the middle of the night. She was listless, too. She didn't seem to have the energy to get the women's study group going. The bright spot in my life was dimming.

There was a strain on me, too, looking back on it, because I watched it all and could do nothing. Even though the doctor in Providence was clear that there wasn't any identifiable threat to her or the baby, we remained in a state of anxiety until Rebbetzin Grossbaum kindly offered that Toba stay with her in Rhode Island for the last two months, at least until the baby came, and then she would be better. Toba reacted very negatively to this idea – Innsmouth was her home now, her calling – but I confess we ganged up on her, aided with a conference call from her mother, until I drove my wife and unborn child to the apparent safety of someone's faraway home. I visited of course, several times a week, but it wasn't the same.

"Your lives are going to change when the baby comes," Rebbetzin Grossbaum assured me. "You can't even begin to guess where you're going to be spiritually a month from now. Hashem has a plan for both of you. There's no reason to fight it because it's the best possible plan."

Looking back now, I have to say that I doubted not the Rebbetzin herself, only her words.

There was a great stillness in the house without Toba. I let my computer play Klezmer music, even a little Matisyahu, just for the background noise. Ironically, I used a noisemaker on my bed stand that played the sound of ocean waves to fall asleep at night. I went into Old Town only by mistake, when I was frustrated by an ensnaring circle of one-way roads. The ocean machine made clean, wholesome waves. I was sure I wouldn't find those anywhere nearby.

This all left me with a surprising amount of time on my hands. The community wasn't large enough for me to be stuck in meetings with congregants – not that I truly had a real shul – and it left me with a lot of hours in the day with an empty house. It was an ideal time to devote myself to study, but my mind wandered. I was waiting, searching for something to fill the hours. I was easily distracted and struggled to get my page of Gemara done each day. I spent hours on the internet looking for anything about Innsmouth and its connection to the Esoteric Order of Dagon, who did seem to worship the Philistine fish god if what few bits of information I found were truth.

When the call came, I didn't want it.

Pavel needed me to come over to his smelly little apartment, immediately. It was already dark, and Innsmouth was always worse in the dark. Maybe something to do with the tides. A small part of me was thrilled that he looked to me as someone of authority, who could be trusted in a time of crisis. Of course I would come, I told him. As fast as I could.

New Town wasn't very big and it was easier just to walk. It was summer, but the air was chilly, and I was happy for all my layers of wool. Pavel's house had no lights in the windows except for one on the first floor. He answered the door and stepped back to invite me in. There were only lamps and a kitchen light to guide me. On the coffee table was a cardboard box.

"Open it," he said and wandered to the kitchen area, where he was backlit by the only good light in the room. I took my seat obediently and removed the dust-covered masking tape that was barely holding the top together.

I could see the glittering before I could position the box for the lamp to properly illuminate it. I had only seen it once before, and in a picture, but I knew that sort of gold, the kind that didn't glitter right. It looked like fake pirate treasure or gelt, because those were the only two situations I'd ever been in where I'd had a chance to see so many gold coins. It wasn't a large box, but it was heavy, and I couldn't see the bottom. Bracelets and a necklace mixed with coins.

"It's for you." Pavel took his seat in the armchair, one arm hanging out of view. He was still in his stained work clothes. "I was going to wait longer, until it seemed like you needed the money, to not be too obvious about it. I want you to see it all so there's no confusion later. The others know." He did not mean the community in general.

"I'm overwhelmed . . . "

"Da, whatever." Pavel shifted in his chair and his right arm came to rest on his leg. I was so entranced by more obvious concerns that I did not at first see the gun. I didn't know what kind of gun it was – some kind of handgun. I must have jumped a little, because he smiled. It was the first time he ever really smiled at me, as if he was really amused, and he had three gold teeth. "Don't worry. This is not for you. The money is. Get whatever you can for it."

I didn't know what to do with the box now, in its tipped position. I didn't want to make any sudden movements. I was so tense I wasn't sure if I could. "Pavel . . ." But I didn't have anything to say, really.

There was no course on this. My eyes were adjusting to the dim light and I could see the stains on his arms and legs were wet. His sleeve was torn on one side and there was blood, but he didn't seem concerned. "We should go to the hospital."

"You really think I am going to a hospital? I suppose you don't know what to think. But you've seen blood before. You used to kill things."

"Chickens," I said. "I killed chickens. In a slaughterhouse."

"Animals." He looked away from me. "My wife, you know, I thought I had more time, because we weren't going to have more children. She was beautiful when I married her. Now, of course, not so much. But she got it in her somehow. I don't know whose child it was going to be. Or what child it was going to be. So I did the decent thing because this all has to stop."

"Where's Mrs. – "

"She's dead, you idiot. She became an animal and she was going to bring another little animals into the world, and I killed her. Because that's what you do to animals." He was angry at me, but not too angry. Not enough for me to duck for cover, if I could actually get my muscles to loosen for a moment. "It's going to happen to all of us. We decided we're not going to wait for them to take to the water. You have to kill them when they're on land. Yuri was the first because he was brave. We buried him in the backyard. My backyard. We had no Rabbi. Now we do."

"Yuri's in Israel."

153

"Da, we told you that."

"He made aliyah after his wife died . . . " And the rest of the sentence, whatever it would have been, just petered out.

Pavel leaned forward as if to whisper to me, even though I could tell we were very, very alone in that house, "You have to kill them with violence. They don't die otherwise. They go to live with Dagon and Mama Hydra. If you don't kill them, it will never stop."

"The Innsmouth folk." I don't know why I said it. This wasn't the time to worry about a little casual racism.

He nodded. "So you understand."

"Barely."

"Enough. And you're not going to try to talk me out of it."

"Out of what?"

With that, Pavel pressed the barrel of the gun to the shiny surface of his bald head and pulled the trigger.

I must have screamed. I remember a scream but not what it sounded like. I was too tense to keep it going for long, though I did finally release my hold on the cardboard box of unholy Innsmouth treasure. Pavel was to my right, and the blood splattered against the wall, in the opposite direction of me.

"Fuck!" I couldn't find my cell phone fast enough. My shaking fingers couldn't manage their way to the 9-1-1 buttons fast enough. Nothing was fast enough, not even the calm operator. I told her I'd just seen a man kill himself and gave the address, and if nothing had happened at all, she told me to wait for the police and not touch anything. Honestly, she could have told me to throw myself out the window and I would have done it. I would have done anything this woman asked of me.

And yet I did not follow her instructions, because as soon I was done, I raced to the kitchen, finding the sink just fast enough to throw up until I was nothing more than a hacking puddle of a man. As I slunk down to the cool floor beneath me, resting my head against the cabinet, the silence reminded me of things. Like how the police were coming. How I was sharing the room with a dead man with a gun and a fortune of gold pieces and jewelry. How his wife was dead, her body somewhere. How my DNA, even if I managed to get out of this somehow, was at least now all over the sink and some of the counter.

How I had just called the Innsmouth police and they didn't care for outsiders.

His wife – where was his wife? He said she was dead but – I knew she lived upstairs. And I knew I wasn't supposed to touch anything, but my general beliefs about the universe were being upended. And I could see that there were specks of blood on the wooden stairs.

Figuring some hasty escape would now put me in a worse position, I ran the sink long enough to wash my mouth out, unbuttoned my collar, and stood at the foot of the stairs I had never climbed or been invited to climb. I wasn't expected to sit in a tiny living room with a dead body, was I? I couldn't even look at the thing that had been Pavel. He was a Jew, and someone needed to stay with him, but the stairs would be the same building. They weren't even very high.

There was nothing of interest on the second floor. Two bedrooms, one converted into a library with a computer, and a bathroom. I wasn't expecting anything, either, because the blood trail continued right up to that attic, with the round window and curtains so heavy across it that you could barely tell the light was on at night. It was darkness now, and I ascended in that darkness. Maybe I wanted it. At the top, some ounce of brain matter told me to hit the light with my shoulder and not my sweaty hands and their fingerprints.

The scene was comforting at first. There were back windows, not visible from the street, but they were boarded up. The rest of the pyramid room was tastefully decorated like my grandmother's, in terms of furniture and accents. The only thing out of place was a half-filled bathtub not connected to any plumbing, and it was the old type with the brass feet. I must have taken in the whole room first out of luck, because once I saw her, I couldn't see anything else.

It was a her, I was fairly sure of it, but only from context. Her gown might have been quite beautiful on a live woman, but it was wet with blood and the bathtub's slimy water. It was hard to see exactly how many shots had been fired into . . . her . . . but the chest was a bloody mess, and there was almost nothing left of her head. Not that I would have made out much of it anyway. She must have died in a struggle, her claws holding onto scraps of cloth from Pavel's shirt. And they were claws at the end of those scaled green limbs. Her legs stuck out as if they were permanently bent, like a frog's. No shoes would have fit on her widened, webbed feet. There was some expression on her, and I recognized the unforgettable, unwinking gaze of the Innsmouth look in the remaining eye staring right back at me.

I screamed again but I didn't hear it. I know I kept screaming until it hurt my throat, even when I muffled it by putting my head on the floor. I was screaming into wood and drawing on my voice alone for protection until there was no more.

***

I was back at Chabad House. I felt my own couch beneath me, and when I opened my eyes, I could see the Rebbe on the wall. He was holding his right hand out in front of him with the tips of his fingers clutching a coin for tzedakah. It was my favorite picture of him.

The room was very bright. The Russians surrounding me – there were only four now – had turned everything on. One of them offered me a glass of water, but they maintained an open vodka bottle on the table.

"The police are coming," I said. I sat up, not yet ready to face them. I put my face in my hands instead.

"Investigators are coming, but they're not the police," said the most fluent Russian. His name was Aron. After I drank the water, they gave me vodka, and I downed more of it than I should have.

"Someone should be with the body," I mumbled.

"What?"

"Pavel – someone should be with his body until he's buried." To their silence I added, "Jewish law. Do you want me to do it?"

One of the others cracked a dark smile. "After all that, you want to honor his body?"

"It doesn't matter what he did. There should be a shomer with the body – a guard. And I have to call the hevra kadisha society in Providence to prepare it for burial."

"You are real Rabbi," Aron said with the same humor. "We didn't doubt it. They're not going to bury him, Rabbi. They're going to feed him to Devil's Reef."

I didn't want to know what that was, so I didn't ask. They would tell me anyway. I looked away from them. The dreaded box was in the corner of the room. A large fortune hidden in disintegrating cardboard.

"Why am I here?"

"In the book of Samuel, it says that when in ancient Israel, when Ark of the Covenant was captured by the Philistines, it was brought to a Temple of Dagon in Ashdod," Aron said, taking a seat on the opposite chair. "The priests went to check on it, and they found the statue of Dagon prostrating to the Ark. They straightened it up, but when they checked that night, it had 'fallen over' again. Prostrating to the Hebrew box. I wasn't raised on biblical stories, but I wasn't raised to believe in fish gods or see their children either."

"Rabbi Grossbaum said it was a Satanic cult," I said, grappling for something substantial. To prove I wasn't a total fool.

"Outsiders don't understand. We didn't understand, or we never would have come here," Aron explained. "This used to be a normal town. Two hundred years ago maybe. But there was famine and one man named Marsh – everything's named after him, you might have noticed – comes from trading across the sea to say he's found a better god than Christ. The real thing. And when they started worshipping it, the fish came in, and they found gold on the shore. And then the god said it wasn't enough to offer human sacrifices – that's what they were doing – but they had to mate with his children, the people who live under the sea. A whole race of deep sea monsters. The children would look normal when they were young, but as they got older they would become like their ancestors, and they would swim home. Their underwater home."

"The government found out," I said, because it was obvious.

"They did everything they could. Tore down the temple. Blew up anything they could find in the water. But it was in the local blood. We didn't know about any of this – we thought we found a strange place with beautiful young women who wanted to marry mean old Russian men, and we would get green cards and inherit fortunes."

They exchanged looks, the four of them.

"They brought up a thing before we got here. It lives in the reef. Now that everything else is gone, it's their only communication with Dagon. A prophet shoggoth, even if it isn't too intelligent."

"We haven't seen it," one of the others clarified. "Yuri did. He wanted to see for himself. He was trying to decide whether to let his wife have her baby. It wasn't his – none of us got them pregnant. They didn't know because we didn't tell them, but we were liquidators at Chernobyl. Cleaning up after the accident. Our team would go deep into the forest to kill stray house pets and animals because their fur had radioactive dust on it. So they decided to get pregnant some other way, and Yuri said he had the right to at least see this servant of Dagon. He went out to Devil's Reef, what's left of it, and he came back and shot his wife and then himself."

"But not before he sent the jewelry to Chabad," I pointed out.

"And we looked at your résumé. We wanted someone who had done kosher slaughter. Someone not faint of heart, if it came to this."

I did not at that moment ask what it had come to. "Why Chabad? Why not just some Israeli manic?

There's a ton of Kabbalists in Safed with military training. They would jump all over this."

"Because you want to spread – how do you say? – yiddishkeit. You want to be here, don't you?"

They were mocking me but it was true. I had wanted to be here. To spend my whole life making this community work. I looked up at the nearest available picture of the Rebbe. It was his mission. I was just an emissary. A soldier for Jewish spirituality. I put up with the bad smell and the hostile locals. Toba would be here right now if she wasn't sick. She was going to come back with our baby, and we were going to start a family.

Aron did not wait for my answer. "If you could only save the other people who've come here, that would be enough. We're already damned. Telling them to leave wouldn't be enough. It wouldn't solve the evil that seeps inside you, hollows you out. Like the invisible radiation in Prypiat. We were supposed to leave that kind of world behind us when we came to America. And now here it is again."

They left me alone, at least for a few moments. There was too much horror. I had to focus.

"Where is Pavel's body now?" I asked.

With utter calm, Aron answered, "They're going to feed it to the shoggoth."

"You can't convince them of otherwise? On religious grounds?"

The laughter was very hollow. "He killed a child of the sea, the unborn next generation when his whole purpose was to produce one. What do you expect?"

I took a little more vodka and indicated I needed time to think. They gave me the time but did not leave. I was too nervous to eat. I couldn't so much as enter the kitchen. I paced the foyer with the old fireplace. We had turned it into a library, with a full set of Talmud and many books in Yiddish and spare siddurs for guests.

For the entire congregation that might have been.

I wrote an email to my wife and a far more explanatory one to Rabbi Grossbaum. Not the full story, certainly, but enough. In fact, I could sum it up in a few lines. The others were helping themselves to my liquor cabinet when I returned.

"The Mishnah says," I explained, "that if gentiles come and demand of our women, 'Give us one and we will defile her and if not we will defile you all,' we should let them defile us all rather than betray one soul from Israel. I know it's a loose interpretation, but I'm going after Pavel."

The night is now unseasonably cold and the ocean winds made my shiver even though I was the one in the wool coat. Aron had borrowed a neighbor's rowboat. Anything else would have made too much noise, he said.

Old Town still had very few working streetlights and there was no moon. I could not see if lights were on at the church by City Hall, but we tried not to worry about that for the time being. We took the back rounds and I saw no one. I was ready for the smell. The silence surprised me. The wharf was a confusing mess of decaying frames of buildings, with no signs to guide a stranger. We used a boathouse for cover while we climbed in and the others pushed us off.

"Can you swim, Rabbi?" Aron finally got around to asking. The ocean, fortunately, was very quiet, and there were a few ships anchored around us.

"I can doggy-paddle," I said.

He said something in Russian. I don't think it was anything good.

It was hard to make out exactly what we were sailing to. The waves lapped at it. It looked like a pile of rubble, with too many odd angles for natural stone. As my eyes adjusted, I could make out that it was probably much larger underneath and would be more visible at low tide. We approached the reef from behind, putting it between us and the shore of Innsmouth, until I could get close enough to touch it and see that it was a natural reef. This was what the government must have dynamited.

"They'll come here after services," Aron said. "I don't know what it's like inside, but there's air. There must be. And there's gold."

"I'll pass."

"I thought you might." He had a little humor in him after all, but he had reason to be steadier than I was. He wasn't getting out of the boat. "You are a brave man. Brave and stupid."

As we waited, I thought I saw lights flickering in the room on the top floor of City Hall.

"My wife is the same as Pavel's now," Aron said. "Almost. She will be soon. She doesn't talk too much anymore. They said if I took another oath, I would be able to understand all that gibbering, but I didn't."

"Jew aren't supposed to take oaths," I told him. "They're too powerful. Always say, 'Maybe, maybe, maybe.'"

"Can I kill her? Is it like killing an animal or killing a man?"

"I don't know. You'd need a better rabbi than me to make that call."

"Maybe they'll send one."

We saw the movement on the shore first, but the bigger crowd was swimming away from us. While the black-cloaked Innsmouth priesthood made their way to the shore, bumps in the waves appeared unconcerned with the ocean's push and pull. It was too dark and they acted too much like water for me to make out what they were, until they emerged on the dock, hunchbacked and dripping with slime. Light enough from the wharf allowed me to see their glistening, bulging eyes before Aron shoved my head down. I barely had time to catch the exchange of a body-shaped bag.

The priest in a gold tiara joined them in the water.

"Don't take them all on," Aron whispered. "Go! Go!"

I don't know what he was imagining I was going to do. I felt around until I found an opening and slid down the tunnel, landing wherever I landed – somewhere dry, at least. All I had was my knife, a hatchet and a pistol I didn't know how to use. I was told it was loaded. Fortunately, I had very little time to second-guess myself before the priest entered from the other direction, and I had to hide in shadows from his torch. He was a bulbous man, but still mostly a man even if his skin was sickly green and his eyes too wide and too large. On Aron's advice I didn't watch the ceremony. I closed my eyes.

Iä! Iä! Cthulhu Fhtagn!

Ph'nglui Mglw'nafh Cthulhu R'lyeh wgah'nagl fhtagn!

Iä! Iä!

They chanted like they were working themselves up to someone or something. It was not the nasally, pronounceable tones I was used to. It sounded like two tongues were needed to say it correctly.

Iä! Iä! Cthulhu Fhtagn!

Hear Oh Israel, the Lord Our G-d, the Lord is One! I said to myself, in my own head, the only time I was ever too afraid to proclaim it. I did not have the brain to review all that had passed, like the flashbacks of a dying person, but I remembered that I had once, earlier in the evening but so long ago, had determination. My G-d was the King of the Universe. He could handle this thing from the deep. These creatures might live for a long time, but He would reign forever and ever.

I was still panicking long after the ceremony died down. My body was too stiff from tension to really move into the now empty room, still lit by the abandoned torch. Pavel's body lay on a slab before the bas relief of a fish head with tentacles for a beard. The monstrosity held his right claw up and open for offering. Beneath him is an opening into watery darkness.

Taking Pavel's body out and hoping that Aron was still there might have been the right thing to do. But Aron knew what things couldn't be left to stand. That was why they called in a religious fanatic like me. Only a self-righteous idiot would remove the bat-winged idol from its stand and break it against the stone wall, then hurl it in the water as an open invitation.

It came first with its tentacles, which were in place of its head. They were almost entirely translucent, and only the angle of the flickering light helped me make out their presence. The quivering body that followed was more of the same, a round pot for a plant-like head. It emerged with a long sucking sound, willing air into its body through gaping pores from all sides of the torso. The feet – if that was all of it and it did not extend indefinitely into the sea – had long toes like tree roots torn from the ground. And yet it was surprisingly nimble. It moved slowly, its pores still inhaling and exhaling with the infernal smacking sounds of a boorish man tasting soup. It was assessing the situation as clearly as I was. The shouggoth, the unholy servant of its unholy master. Pavel's body, an unclean thing. Me.

It had no eyes, yet we stared at each other all the same.

It's breathing heavily now. It's breathing at me because it's alive longer that it should be, longer than it ever should have been. No one ever should have tolerated this existence. Its tentacles wiggle as it takes long, gaping breaths of still cave air, and all I can think is that it has many necks to cut.

***

To Our Beloved Friends and Family,

Today we light a candle for the first yartzeit of Rabbi Menachem Schneuri, who died in a tragic boating accident while serving the Jewish community in Innsmouth, Massachusetts. Rabbi Schneuri is remembered as a kind and gentle soul who was beloved by his small but fast-growing congregation. Also lighting a candle are his wife and newborn son, Noam Schneuri.

Please take a moment to honor this luminary who committed his brief life to Yiddishkeit and the sanctification of Hashem's name. While the community of Innsmouth remembers him, we must remember them. Consider a contribution to the Chabad House of Innsmouth, care of Aron Zaslavsky, Allen Street, Zip Code 09812.

Author Bios

Megan Arkenberg a Wisconsin native, now lives and writes in California. Her work has appeared in *Asimov's, Lightspeed, Strange Horizons,* and dozens of other places. She won the 2012 Rhysling Award in the long form category and the 2013 Asimov's Readers' Award for best short story. Megan procrastinates by editing the fantasy e-zine *Mirror Dance*.

Jeff Chapman writes software by day and speculative fiction when he should be sleeping. His tales range from fantasy to horror and they don't all end badly. He lives with his wife, children, and cats in a house with more books than bookshelf space. You can find him musing about words and fiction at jeffchapmanwriter.blogspot.com.

Lyda Morehouse has made a career of writing about those things you're not supposed to mention in polite company: religion, politics, and sex. Her novel Archangel Protocol, recently re-released as an e-book by Wizard's Tower Press, won the 2001 Shamus for best paperback original featuring a private eye. Apocalypse Array, the last novel in the AngeLINK tetrology (which includes Fallen Host and Messiah Node) won the Philip K. Dick Special Citation for Excellence. She's also published several paranormal romances as Tate Hallaway. You can find out more about Lyda at: http://www.lydamorehouse.com

Marsha Morman is the author of too many books of Regency fiction under the name Marsha Altman and not enough speculative fiction. She has a BA from Brown University and an MFA from the City College of New York. She is working on a novel of Tibetan science fiction. Marsha will continue writing because otherwise she might have to work for a living, or at least leave her apartment. She does not own any cats.

Alter Reiss is a scientific editor and field archaeologist. He lives in Jerusalem with his wife Naomi and their son Uriel, and enjoys good books, bad movies, and old time radio shows. Alter's fiction has appeared in Strange Horizons, the Magazine of Fantasy and Science Fiction, and elsewhere."

Romie Stott is an editor of the slipstream magazine *Reflection's Edge*. Her work has been published by *Strange Horizons*, *Jerseyworks*, *The Huffington Post*, and *Death List Five*, among others. As a filmmaker (working under the name Romie Faienza), she has displayed work at the National Gallery in London and the Dallas Museum of Art, and participated in Jonathan Lethem's Promiscuous Materials Project. She is a founding member of the film and art collective Rocker Box Gasket.

Sonya Taaffe's short stories and poems have appeared in such venues as *Beyond Binary: Genderqueer and Sexually Fluid Speculative Fiction*, *The Moment of Change: An Anthology of Feminist Speculative Poetry*, *Here, We Cross: A Collection of Queer and Genderfluid Poetry from Stone Telling*, *People of the Book: A Decade of Jewish Science Fiction & Fantasy*, *Last Drink Bird Head*, *The Year's Best Fantasy and Horror*, *The Alchemy of Stars: Rhysling Award Winners Showcase*, and *The Best of Not One of Us*. Her work can be found in the collections *Postcards from the Province of Hyphens* and *Singing Innocence and Experience* (Prime Books) and *A Mayse-Bikhl* (Papaveria Press). She is currently senior poetry editor at *Strange Horizons*; she holds master's degrees in Classics from Brandeis and Yale and once named a Kuiper belt object.

Acknowledgments

First I would like to thank Jay Lake, Michael Fromowitz, David Guttierez and Avi Cohen for helping with Dybbuk Press at the beginning. Steve Berman, Carlton Mellick III and Jeff Burk have all provided guidance on how to run a successful independent publishing house.

The following people donated money and publicity to the Indiegogo Campaign – Emilia Cataldo, Beckett Horowitz, Gordon Davidescu, Adrienne Jones, Joline Zepcevski, Jeanette Pontier, Michael Lee, Marie Middleton, Leah Linzmeier Anderson, Jesper Rudgard Jensen, Richard Rosenbaum, Elazer Nuddell, William Brock, Jesse Keenan, Sheri Halverson, Bill Olver, Jeffrey Culver, and Dovid Smith.

This book comes from a long standing affection for Tanakh as a literary tradition. Various teachers have guided me in my studies including Rabbi Yosi Gordon, Rabbi Stephen Belsky, Rabbi Max Davis, Rabbi Barry Dolinger, Professor Tsvi Zahavey, Rabbi Hayyim Angel, and Robert Alter.

CPSIA information can be obtained
at www.ICGtesting.com
Printed in the USA
BVHW04s0001250618
519716BV00005B/32/P

9 780976 654681